Facing Fears

A River's End Ranch Story

Kirsten Osbourne

Sign up for instant notification of all of Kirsten's New Releases Text 'BOB' to 42828

And

For a complete list of Kirsten's works head to her website wwww.kirstenandmorganna.com

Chapter One

Gabriella Tanner stepped out of the car she'd ridden in from the Lewiston airport on shaky legs. She thanked the driver—mostly for not killing her as he drove the hairpin curves of the mountains at a faster pace than anyone should have survived. Of course, if she'd had to drive it, she'd have gone twenty miles per hour the whole way, and she knew the drivers who were stuck behind her would not have been happy.

"When will you need a ride back to the airport, miss?" the man asked. He was a professional driver with a limo service, and he was obviously all about providing the best service to his clients that he could.

"I'm not certain. My agent will be in touch with you." It felt so strange to say that. She had an agent! She'd graduated from college in December, and someone had specifically asked for her to audition for this show. It was a television series set in the late 1800s called *Legacy*. She wasn't sure she was a good fit, but apparently someone had seen her in her university's production of *Seven Brides for Seven Brothers,* and one thing had led to another. This was now her third audition, and it was on the set on River's End Ranch. She just hoped she didn't have a heart attack before she got to that point.

The driver took her bags from the back of the car and carried them into the lobby of the small hotel. She stepped up to the desk. "I have reservations. My name is Gabriella Tanner."

The man behind the desk nodded. "Of course, Miss Tanner. I just need to see some identification. There's already an account set up for you for incidentals."

"Yes, thank you." She dug in her purse for her ID, handing it to him. "Is it possible for me to get a room on the first floor?"

"We don't have any available. I'm very sorry. I could see about putting you into a cabin instead . . ."

She shook her head. She couldn't afford to pay the difference if she didn't get the part. "No, thank you. I'll manage."

"If it's an accessibility issue, we do have an elevator . . ."

"No, it's not, but thank you." She had no problems climbing stairs . . . she just had problems being high up. Even just looking out the window would make her very nervous. What she was doing auditioning for a show that took place in the mountains, she didn't know. Hopefully, they'd never ask her to film anywhere at a higher elevation than she was now. Her ears were popping where they were. She wasn't sure she could handle that.

The man eyed her for a moment before nodding. "Your room is at the top of the stairs and to the right." He pulled a basket out from under the counter. "This is for you. I hope you enjoy your stay. If you need anything else, don't hesitate to call." He nodded to another young man who was standing off to one side. "Would you show Miss Tanner to her room?"

The man nodded. "Yes, of course. Right this way." He led her toward the elevator, pulling her suitcase for her, while she followed with her gift basket.

She could see some Frank's Fudge under the wrapping, and she couldn't wait to sink her teeth into it. She'd had it a couple of times for special occasions, and she knew it was the best chocolate available in the US.

She was put into a room that wasn't your average hotel room. It felt more like a bedroom she'd be given as a member of the family. She had a private bath and a big closet. It would be perfect. She knew it was down to just two women for the heroine of the show, and she hoped she got it with everything inside her. Of course, going against Sierra Barker was nerve-wracking. Sierra was a big name, while Gabby was just a nobody fresh from college. Why, she hadn't even planned to go into acting, and she didn't know what she was doing there.

She took deep breaths, closing her eyes as she pulled the drapes closed. She couldn't have a panic attack now. Not when she'd just gotten to River's End Ranch, the place where the real-life story had happened and where the show would be filmed. She had two days to wander around the ranch and get her bearings before the audition. She had the script—though she hadn't looked at it yet. She'd auditioned twice already to play Frankie, a young girl who lied about both her age and her sex to move out west with her brother and homestead.

She sat down on the bed and pulled a brochure about the ranch closer to her, hoping there was somewhere she could eat. There had to be a restaurant or two. She looked through and found a diner called Kelsey's Kafé. There was a map to get there, so she decided to head over. It sounded like the informal meal she was looking for as she got to know the people of the ranch. Getting a feel for the people would surely help her in the audition.

Walking toward the diner, she looked around at the beautiful ranch. There were little signs pointing the way to everything. One was to the diner and the spa, which she would definitely be checking out if she got the part, and another was to the Old West Town. That was probably where they'd be filming, so she would check it out after lunch. She was glad she'd flown in so early in the day, so she could have time to look around and see what she could see.

Once she got to the diner, she looked at it with a smile. It seemed to have been built in the fifties. Inside, she saw a blond woman chatting with a man in a sheriff's uniform. The blonde looked over at her with a smile. "Hi, I'm Kelsi. Table for one?"

"Yes, please." The diner looked pretty empty other than the sheriff.

"You came at the perfect time. After the breakfast rush and before the lunch rush. My husband likes to do his paperwork here sometimes!" Kelsi led Gabby over to a table. "You here for a bit?"

Gabby nodded. "I'm auditioning for the show. This is my third audition, and they flew me out here for it. I'm super nervous."

Kelsi's face lit up. "My family owns the ranch, and it was one of our ancestors who settled here! Are you auditioning for Frankie? Or one of the lesser parts?"

"Frankie." Gabby couldn't help but wonder if the other woman had any say in who was cast. Not that she'd try to sway her in any way because she still wasn't sure if acting was what she wanted to do. . . .

"I think you have the look for her." Kelsi clapped her hands together. "I'm so excited that it's finally starting! We've been working to get the ranch ready. It's getting real now that actors are showing up!"

Gabby smiled, feeling like the other woman's enthusiasm was contagious. "I'm planning to explore the ranch today. Maybe spend some time in the Old West Town. I really want to get a feel for this place."

"You're going to love it here! We have the best tourist ranch ever!" Kelsi glanced over as a man entered the diner. "Noah, are you working today?"

Noah shook his head. "Nah. I'm off. Does that mean you won't feed me?"

"You know I'll always feed you. Come meet someone!" When Noah walked over to Gabby's table, Kelsi said, "Noah this is Gabby. Gabby's auditioning for one of the lead roles in the new show, and she needs someone to show her around the ranch. What do you think?"

Noah blinked at Kelsi for a moment. "What do I think about what?"

"What do you think about showing her around? Lunch is on me today if you will!"

Gabby shook her head. "Oh, you don't have to do that!"

Noah shrugged. "Sure. You know I'll do anything for a free lunch. I'll take whatever Bob's special of the day is, and I want it doubled. I'm starving." He slipped into the booth across from Gabby and grinned at her. "Bob's specials are always worth eating, so I say you order the same. You don't have to have double it, though, but since I'm buying your lunch and Kelsi is putting it all on the house, you might as well."

Kelsi didn't even argue. "He's right. Bob can cook like nobody's business, but we don't tell him because he gets all big-headed about it!"

"I heard that!" Bob said, sticking his head out of the kitchen. "I thought I was done getting picked on now that Joni's gone!"

"You just keep dreaming, Bob. As long as there are waitresses at Kelsey's Kafé, there will be people to pick on you. Deal with it!" Kelsi grinned at Gabby. "You want to try his special? It's Salisbury steak and mashed potatoes with carrots today. Doesn't sound fabulous, but trust me . . . it's to die for!"

Gabby bit her lip, worried about gaining weight if she was going to be on television. "Maybe I should just have a salad. . . ."

Kelsi looked at her. "You're beautiful, and Noah is going to walk you all over this ranch later today. You'll work it off."

Gabby was surprised the other woman understood her so well with so few words. "All right, you've convinced me. Salisbury steak it is."

As soon as Kelsi hurried off, Gabby looked over at Noah. "I won't tell her if you don't want to give me the tour. You'll still get your free lunch."

He shook his head. "No, I'm not about to renege. I have the chance to spend the day with a pretty girl and show off the most beautiful corner of God's green earth I call home. Why would I back out?"

She blushed. "I just don't want to fill up your day on your day off."

"Gives me something constructive to do. I was going to take a snowmobile into the mountains, and there's no better way to see the ranch. We can do that together."

Gabby felt her stomach clench at the mere thought. "I can't do that."

He frowned. "Why not? It's fun!"

She looked around, making sure no one was listening. "I'm afraid of heights."

"Oh, that? I can help you get over that!"

"No, not me. It's a full-fledged phobia. I have dreams that I'm falling all the time. Off buildings, down mountains, off bridges. It's crazy. I can't even drive a car over a bridge without having a panic attack." Gabby brushed her long dark hair away from her face. "I shouldn't admit it, and I hope it won't keep me from getting the part, but I'd appreciate it if you'd keep that between us."

"What will the part entail?" he asked, frowning. "If you're filming here at the ranch, there will likely be some scenes in the mountains."

"I hope not." She bit her lip, not wanting to give up on the idea . . . she didn't think. She still wasn't sure if she wanted to act or go to graduate school for her CPA. One was definitely the wiser choice, but the other . . . well, it had always been a dream.

"Maybe I can help you. We can go up a little today, but not far. Then I'll work with you while you're here. Gradually working up further and further."

"I'm not sure about that . . . I think I'll just freak out." Gabby had never been able to even climb a ladder, let alone go up a mountain.

"We can try, though, can't we?"

"You promise to bring me right back down if I get scared?" she asked, still worried.

"I promise. Do I need to write an oath in blood? Cross my heart and hope to fall off a mountain?"

"Do people fall off mountains?"

Noah grinned. "Only if they're really stupid and don't pay attention." He refrained from mentioning that it had just happened a couple of months before.

She sighed. "I guess we'll try. If you really will bring me right down if I get scared."

"I said I would!"

Kelsi stopped at the table then, putting their food in front of them. "I forgot to ask what you wanted to drink, so I brought water. Noah, I'm sure you'll want something else because it's free today."

"Of course, I do! I'll have a root beer."

"Gabby?"

"Water is fine with me," Gabby replied, looking at the huge lunch in front of her. She was sure she couldn't eat it all, and Noah had two of them. "Do you always eat two lunches?"

"Yup. I'm a growing boy!"

Gabby studied him for a moment, certain he was at least a couple of years older than her twenty-two. "How old are you?"

"Old enough to know better, but still young enough to try it!"

She laughed at his light-hearted attitude as Kelsi came back with his drink. "I think I'm going to like spending the day with you."

"I sure hope so. I'm planning on forcing you to spend the evening with me, too. It's trivia night at the restaurant, and I need my team to win this week."

"And you think I can make that happen?" she asked, taking a bite of her mashed potatoes. "Bob really can cook!"

"Yeah, he's good," Kelsi replied. "Enjoy and let me know if you need anything else."

"She seems really nice. Is everyone in the family so warm?" Gabby asked.

"Kelsi's pretty special, even among the Westons. I'm one of the assistants to Wes Weston. He's the guy in charge of rock climbing and skiing. If it happens on one of the mountains, we're involved."

"Do you enjoy that?" She couldn't imagine someone liking to be on a mountain every day, but if it was something he enjoyed, she certainly wouldn't say anything.

"I love every minute of every day. I grew up not far from here, and my parents vacationed at River's End every single summer. We did a lot of Christmas breaks here, too. I guess being up on those mountains reminds me of all the good times I had with my family as a kid."

"You don't have good times with them anymore?"

He shook his head. "My mom died of breast cancer when I was a teenager. My dad remarried, and his wife was never really interested in my brother or me, so we moved on. They have kids together now, and it just doesn't feel the same."

"I'm sorry." And she was. She'd always been very close to her parents and her younger brother. "My family is super close."

"Do I detect a bit of a southern accent in your voice?" he asked, his eyes dancing.

"Well, maybe. I thought I'd managed to hide it completely, but is it really possible to hide the south in your voice? I grew up in Southern Louisiana, not too far north of New Orleans."

"Interesting. An area I've always wanted to visit, but I've never really had the opportunity." He cut off a piece of steak from his second plate. That's when she realized he'd already polished off his first plate completely. "Did you always want to be an actress?"

She shrugged. "I went to school for accounting, and I always thought I'd be a CPA. I did some of the shows at school just as a lark, and during my last one, someone saw me. I still don't know who, but they asked me specifically to audition for this show. I still don't even know if I want to be an actress. I might just want to sit in a dreary office playing with numbers all day."

He laughed. "Oh, you want to be an actress. It's right there on your face when you talk about theater. I think you'd be a good one, too!"

"I guess. I'm up against some tough competition for the part though, and a nobody like me beating out Sierra Barker would be miraculous." She pushed her half-eaten food away from her.

Noah finished his second steak and glanced at her plate. "Are you going to finish that?"

She shook her head. "No, have at it if you're really that hungry."

"Starving. I'm always starving. My mother used to say I had a tape worm to be able to eat as much as I do and never gain weight, but I work it all off. If there's physical labor to be done, I'm your man. I love working with my hands."

"How long have you worked here?"

He swallowed the bite of food in his mouth—the last one from her plate—before answering. "Ten years. I came here right after high school, and because the Weston family already knew me and knew how good I was on the mountain, they hired me right away. I started as just another man on the team, but I've worked my way up to being Wes's assistant. It's a good job, and I'm happy doing it."

"I can't imagine working anywhere for ten years." She sipped her water. "My mother is an English teacher, and she has worked with the same school district since before I was born. She keeps saying she's going to retire in a year or two, but it never happens. She loves what she does too much to ever actually stop. They'll be carrying her out of the school in a body bag someday."

"What does your father do?"

"He's a lawyer. He used to work for a big law firm out of New Orleans, but Mama has always worked in St. Tammany Parish. He didn't like the commute, and she wasn't about to go work in a big city school, so he opened his own practice in Slidell. That's where I grew up."

"Sounds like you liked it there."

"Oh, I did. It was a good medium-sized town to grow up in. Small enough that kids could play in the streets and not worry too much, but big enough we had a shopping mall and theaters. Lots of things to do."

"Did you go to college near there?" he asked, frowning.

"I went to LSU. Bigger city. Bigger school. Competition was fierce there, but I loved it. I was accepted to grad school in Texas, but then I was asked to do this audition. . . . My scholarship will be waiting if I decide to go back to school in the fall. Lots of decisions to make before that." And lots of fears to face. Being an accountant would be an easy out for her. She was good with numbers, and she would have a nice safe life. But was safe what she really needed?

Chapter Two

After lunch, Noah led Gabby to the Old West Town because she made it clear that was the area of the ranch she was most interested in. As they walked, he frowned at her. "Is that the heaviest coat you've got? I know it's March, but you're in Idaho, not Louisiana!"

"Back in Louisiana, girls are laying out to get their tans ready for summer already. Here, I'm shivering in my heaviest coat!"

Noah frowned. "You need to get something that will keep you warmer. We'll start at the General Store." Without thinking about what he was doing, he grabbed her hand and tugged her toward the store, where he still managed everything, deciding what to order. "Heidi always keeps some heavy coats in stock or we can get you a sweater to wear under your coat. Either way, you're going to be way too cold to run around in that light jacket."

Gabby followed along behind him, trying to tug her hand from his. The only time she'd ever really held hands with a man was during plays and for rehearsals. It felt strange to do it without a reason, but it was a good strange, and one she wasn't sure she was ready for. She followed him into the store and stopped. "Wow! I expected to see more old things. This place is amazing!"

Heidi ducked out from behind a clothing rack. "We try to provide everything people forget. We don't want people to have to take their business to Riston now, do we?"

Gabby smiled. "I love your outfit. Is that from the period the ranch would have been settled?"

"Yes, it is. It's late 1880s to early 1890s pioneer dress. Frankie would have worn things like this after she married Wally." Heidi spun in a little circle for Gabby to see her dress.

"Do you wear the shoes, too?" Gabby had always laughed at her friends because they were drooling over the latest shoe styles. To her a good pair of sneakers was all that mattered. Hopefully if she got the part, she'd be able to wear tennis shoes under her dress where they wouldn't show!

Heidi nodded, lifting up her skirt a bit. "They're not the most comfortable shoes in the world, but they look good with the dress."

Gabby grinned. "I'm Gabby. I'm trying out for the show."

"Oh, that's wonderful! We're really looking forward to having the show filmed here. Do you need something today or are you just out exploring?" Heidi seemed genuinely excited to meet her.

"I need something warmer to wear. I brought my heaviest coat, but Noah is complaining that it's not warm enough for Idaho."

"Oh my! Where are you from?" Heidi asked, walking toward her coat section.

"Louisiana. I wear a coat this heavy two or three days a year." Gabby pursed her lips at the coat selection. "I think maybe I just want a sweater that I can wear under my coat. If I don't get the part, I don't want to be stuck with a really thick coat I'll never wear."

Heidi nodded, eyeing Gabby's size and grabbing something from a rack. "This should fit perfectly. You're what? A size one?"

Gabby nodded. "Though I might not be if I keep eating Bob's lunches. I had the Salisbury steak today, and it was wonderful! Good thing Noah ate half of it."

"And he probably had two of his own lunches, right?" Heidi shook her head at Noah, lowering her voice so he wouldn't hear. "Are you two starting something?"

Gabby's eyes grew wide, and she shook her head emphatically. "No, not at all. Kelsi bribed him with a free lunch if he'd show me around the ranch."

Heidi laughed. "That man eats more than any human being I've ever known. It's almost an Olympic sport for him!"

Gabby pulled off her coat and pulled the sweater on, feeling the soft yarn used. She was able to pull her coat on over it as well. "I think this is perfect." She was almost afraid to look and see how much, but she knew she could charge it to the room. Her agent had made it clear that she was to buy anything that made her comfortable. She didn't want to take advantage, but she was an unpaid intern for a CPA office between semesters. Or she was about to be the star of a primetime television show. It was hard to know which!

After charging the sweater to her account, she thanked Heidi for her time, following Noah out the door and immediately stopping to put the sweater on. "Where next?"

"Next we have to go to the bakery. Miranda runs the place. She's Bob's wife, and she bakes as well as he cooks."

"This place is going to put fifteen pounds on me overnight!"

Noah laughed. "Let's do this. Miranda always has a deal where you buy three cookies and get one free. I'll get four, and you can have half of one."

Gabby grinned. "I have to wonder where you're putting all that food . . ."

"People have been wondering that for many years. I wish I had answers." Noah opened the door to a bakery, calling out to the woman behind the counter. "How're you feeling today, Miranda? Little Bob Junior giving you fits?"

Miranda made a face. "I'm not calling him Bob Junior, and I don't care if that's what Bob told you. No more Bobs are needed around here."

Noah shrugged. "That's not what Bob says." He squatted down to look in the display case. "I'm starving."

"What? Did you only have two and a half lunches today instead of three?" Miranda asked, knowing Noah's propensity for eating anything that didn't move.

"Yes!" He said with a groan. "I ordered two lunches, and I ate half of Gabby's, but I didn't get dessert. That's where you come in." He stood up, gesturing to Gabby with his thumb. "This is Gabby. She's one of the actors here to try out for the show. Gabby, this is Miranda, and she's going to give us cookies."

Miranda grinned. "Of course I am. What kind are you hungry for?"

Noah looked again. "I want peanut butter, white chocolate macadamia, and chocolate chip." Glancing over his shoulder, he asked Gabby, "What about you?"

Gabby moved closer and looked into the display case. If she only got to have half a cookie, she was going to make that half a cookie count. "I want a lemonade cookie. They look good!"

Miranda wrapped up the four cookies. "It's nice of you to let her have your free cookie, Noah. Very generous."

"She gets *half* of my free cookie. I'm not nearly as generous as you think I am! Get us each a bottle of water, too."

"I'll pay for my own water," Gabby said, digging into her purse.

"Are you kidding? Kelsi sent us to do this. I'll pay and take her the receipts." Noah winked at her, and Gabby couldn't help but laugh. "She won't even mind!"

Miranda took Noah's credit card and gave him a receipt. "Making the most of the Westons' generosity, I see."

"Well, sure! Kelsi knew what to expect when she asked me!" There were two things everyone knew about Noah. He was always hungry, and he was cheap.

"You taking her to trivia night so you can get free pizza, too?" Miranda asked.

"Shh . . . don't tell her my strategy! She'll think I'm cheap!"

Miranda looked at Gabby. "No matter what anyone tells you, Noah is very cheap. Especially where food is concerned."

Gabby grinned. "I'm starting to get that impression."

"He's a good guy, though, so don't hold it against him . . . too much."

Noah glared at Miranda. "I'm getting her out of here before you tell her all of my secrets!"

"Everyone knows you're cheap, Noah. It's not a secret!" Miranda called as he opened the door.

"Well, it was still a secret from Gabby! Now she knows everything there is to know about me!"

"I'm not sure that's true," Gabby said, waving at Miranda. "I like this Old West Town of yours. Where to next?"

"Oh, the saloon. Sadie does specialty coffees, hot chocolate, ice cream . . . we'll get another dessert from her."

Gabby shook her head. "I think I'll just watch you eat this one." She wasn't even a little bit hungry, and she had half a cookie to eat.

"Might be smart. You don't look like you're ready to eat like I do. You're a lightweight."

"I definitely am compared to you. I think I might gain weight just watching you eat everything you want to eat."

He wrinkled his nose at her. "Are you always this self-conscious about your weight?"

"Not at all. I just don't eat a lot because I don't get that hungry. This week, I'm nervous because of the audition."

"I can understand that. I think you have a better personality for Frankie . . . at least how she was in the book. Have you read the book?" Noah asked as he escorted her to the saloon.

She shook her head. "I haven't. I just found out it was based on a book yesterday. Are you telling me you've read a romance novel?"

He nodded. "And I'm not even ashamed of it. A local romance writer who married one of the men who used to work with the horses here on the ranch wrote it. Pastor Kevin did all the research."

"Pastor Kevin?"

"Yeah, he's the local pastor. He does weddings and stuff. There's a Sunday service at the little chapel here in the old town." Noah gestured toward the chapel, the bag of cookies dangling from his hand.

"Sounds like a good guy. I can't believe all these buildings are really stores and used."

"Well, not all of them are, but a good portion. We even have a working blacksmith here on the property." He led her to the saloon and opened the door. "This is actually a coffee shop and ice cream shop primarily. I love how creative the Westons have gotten with the town buildings and the businesses that go into them."

They walked over and bellied up to the bar of an old-time-looking saloon. "I feel like I should order a sarsaparilla!" Gabby said with a grin.

A woman came around the counter with a smile on her face. "You sure can if that's what you want!"

"I'm actually not sure if I want anything. I think I'll just watch Noah eat or drink or whatever he's decided to do here."

"I'm Sadie, and the saloon is my space."

Gabby nodded. "I'm Gabby."

"She's here to audition for *Legacy!*" Noah said. "Kelsi bribed me with a free lunch to take her around the ranch and introduce her. Gabby wants to get a feel for the place before she auditions."

"I heard Sierra was going to get the lead. Is that not true?" Sadie asked, leaning on the counter.

"There are two of us left auditioning, and the other person is Sierra," Gabby admitted. "I'm nervous about going up against someone so glamorous!"

"Just remember to be yourself. Frankie was not glamorous in any way shape or form. She was a hard worker, determined to do a man's work if she could. She's a legend around here. Well, she wasn't before Kaya's book, but she is now."

"Where can I get my hands on the book?" Gabby asked. She really wanted to read it and get an idea of what everyone else knew about the character she was auditioning for.

Sadie pulled a book out from under the counter. "I keep a few on hand for anyone interested. Kaya is a great writer. I think you'll enjoy it."

Gabby looked at the cover, surprised that the title wasn't *Legacy*. She didn't know why she'd thought the show would have the same name, but she did. Instead it was titled, *Mail Order Miracle*. Interesting. "Thank you! Can I charge it to my room?"

Noah shook his head. "Nah. I'll charge it and give Kelsi the bill."

"She's never going to have you do something like this again, is she?" Gabby asked him.

"No idea. It's kind of fun, though." Noah ordered a hot chocolate and an ice cream.

"Only you, Noah," Sadie said as she wandered off to fix his order.

"What do you think of this place so far?" he asked.

"It's amazing! I can see why they want to do the show here. It fits with the theme, and it's all so beautiful. I wasn't sure I wanted the part until about fifteen minutes ago, but I do. I'm not going to hide for the rest of my life in a dreary office playing with other people's money. I'm going to play Frankie Weston!" Gabby looked down at the book in her hand. "I'll read this after trivia tonight." *Or before if I can squeeze it in!*

"You'll like it. How's your room? You comfortable?" he asked.

"Yeah, it's nice. I wish I wasn't on the second floor, but I'm managing. I shut the curtains, and that helped."

"You can't see the view with the curtains shut!" Noah protested. "Oh, I need you to come up on the mountain with me so you can see it all."

"I'm really not sure I can. I know it's nothing to someone like you, but for me to go up on a mountain is ridiculously frightening."

He frowned. "How 'bout I just show you some pictures I've taken from up there today, and we ease into that? It's going to take the rest of the afternoon to see the Old West Town anyway."

Sadie put his ice cream and hot chocolate in front of him, taking his credit card and ringing him up. "I put the book on your bill."

"Perfect," Noah responded. "Do you mind if I sit here and eat my ice cream?" he asked Gabby. "I will definitely make a mess if I try to walk with it."

"No, I don't mind." Gabby fingered the spine of the book, wondering if he would be offended if she opened it and started reading. She loved to read, and she didn't necessarily enjoy being around a lot of people. She wasn't the type of person who went into acting, but when opportunity knocked, she couldn't exactly ignore it!

Noah watched her touching the book. "Okay, Gabby. It's going to take me about ten minutes to eat this, and then I'll be ready to go. I bet you can make it through the first chapter."

"I don't want to be rude . . ."

He laughed. "You do, too! You just don't want me to think you're being rude, and I won't."

She grinned at him. "Thanks."

"No problem."

She opened the book and found herself sucked into River's End Ranch in 1890.

Noah chatted with Sadie while Gabby read, and he ate two of his cookies along with his ice cream. "It's been twenty minutes. Let's keep exploring."

Gabby wanted to groan. "I like this book! I don't even read romance, and I'm already dying to know what happens."

"Yup. That's what we all said, too." He waited 'til she marked her page with a bookmark that had been stuck in the book, obviously there to advertise Kaya Taylor and her books just a little bit more. "Let's go meet the author's twin sister."

"Wait . . . really? The author has a twin who's around here, too?" Gabby was starting to feel like River's End Ranch was a place she never wanted to leave. Never had she met so many kind, generous people who genuinely wanted her to enjoy herself. She wondered how the ranch hired people who were all so kind and friendly.

As they walked, Noah pointed out different things. "Here we are. The apothecary shop."

"Ooh . . . can we get snake oil?"

He opened the door, and she found she was slightly disappointed. Instead of an apothecary shop, there was a small first aid station. A short brunette walked over to them, her belly slightly rounded. She must be pregnant as well. For a fleeting moment, Gabby wondered what they were going to do when all of the women on the ranch were off for maternity leave.

The brunette smiled. "Which one of you is hurt?"

"Neither one, Bridget. This is Gabby, and she's trying out for Frankie in the show," Noah told her.

Bridget studied her for a moment. "You're up against Sierra Barker. That would scare me."

Gabby smiled. "It scares me, too. She's a big-name actress whom everyone loves, and I'm just a nobody from Louisiana."

"I'm sure you'll do great." Bridget nodded at the book in Gabby's hands. "Read it. I think you'll understand the history of the ranch a lot better. Besides, the book is good. My sister wrote it."

"Noah was just telling me you're Kaya's twin. Are you two identical?"

"I can tell you've never met my sister." Bridget laughed. "Kaya is a full foot taller than me, and she has blond hair. We're as fraternal as twins can be."

"Is that good or bad?"

Bridget shrugged. "Good, I think. We're very different people, and if we were identical, I think it would annoy both of us." She tilted her head to one side for a moment as if she was thinking. "Who's your favorite Disney Princess?"

"My favorite Disney Princess?" Gabby asked. What an odd question to ask someone when you first met them. "Probably Belle. The remake of *Beauty and the Beast* was just incredible. What about you?"

"Cinderella. You can be Kaya's friend." Bridget walked back to where she'd been sitting at a desk and got back to what she'd been doing.

Gabby looked at Noah with wide eyes. "She takes her Disney Princesses very seriously . . ." he explained softly.

"I see that." Gabby wasn't sure what to think, but she wouldn't complain. Obviously, the girl had opinions. "Where to next?"

"Let's go see Bridget's husband!" Noah didn't let himself be bothered by Bridget's moodiness. She'd always been a bit of an odd duck, and now she was pregnant, and it was sure to only get worse.

"You lead!"

Chapter Three

By the time Noah dropped her back at the main house, Gabby was exhausted. She'd gotten up very early for her flight, knowing it was best if she flew when she was half-asleep so she wouldn't panic quite as much. She usually drove anywhere she was going, but there hadn't been time. "I'll pick you up here in an hour and a half for trivia."

"Do I need to dress up?" she asked. She hadn't brought more than one nice outfit, and that was for her audition on Saturday.

"Nope. Jeans and a sweater would be fine." Noah couldn't believe just how attracted to her he was. He had taken the assignment for the free food, of course, but he'd enjoyed himself a great deal more than he'd expected to. "We're going to hook up with my friend Paislee for trivia. We need to see if we can find one more person."

Gabby hadn't realized he had a girlfriend. It was a good thing she was there for purposes that did not include getting involved with a random man assigned to take her around the ranch. "Sounds good. I don't know anyone, though, so you might have to choose our fourth."

A woman stopped. "Wait are you two doing that trivia night thing I've heard about? I want in!" She had purple hair and beautiful green eyes. "I'm Lachele Simpson."

Noah studied her for a moment, surprised that she was willing to invite herself. "That would be fine. Are you here alone, Miss Simpson?"

"Dr. Simpson, but everyone just calls me Dr. Lachele. I'm not here alone, but my husband has to watch basketball tonight, so he'll be no good to any of us. He's going to sit in our room and vegetate." Dr. Lachele shook her head. "Why bother to leave New York and come to a beautiful place like this if you're just going to sit around in your underwear in the room? I don't know what his problem is!"

Noah grinned, finding himself liking this woman. "We're happy to have you on our team, Dr. Lachele. Meet us here in an hour." Maybe having a chaperone would keep him from making a fool of himself over Gabby.

Gabby waved goodbye. "I'll be waiting."

"Good. I don't want to be late." Noah hurried off, and Gabby stood there, clutching her book to her chest.

Dr. Lachele's eyes landed on the book Gabby was holding. "I know the author of that book! I set one of her friends up with a man, and they met at the altar. Kaya is a little insane, especially when she's around her twin sister, Bridget."

"I met Bridget today. She wanted to know who my favorite Disney Princess was . . ."

"Yeah, Bridget's an odd duck. I met them both through their friend, Jenni. I'm just glad they didn't throw each other off that cruise ship we were on in between stabbing each other with shrimp forks." Dr. Lachele headed for the stairs. "I'll see you in an hour. Bring your brain!" She laughed as she walked away, leaving Gabby staring at her. The woman had obviously lost her mind.

The man who had been behind the front desk when she'd checked in walked over to her then. "I have a letter for you," he said. She noted that his name was Owen. She hadn't noticed earlier because she'd been too close to the life-harrowing experience that had been her drive from the airport to the ranch.

"Thank you." Gabby accepted the letter and walked toward the elevator, not letting herself think about how high up she'd be.

When she got to her room, she set an alarm on her phone for forty-five minutes, and then she opened her book and continued reading. It had been a good day, and she'd learned a lot about the ranch, but the book was her favorite thing she'd acquired. Well, her book and the sweater.

Noah was waiting for her downstairs when she arrived for trivia night. Dr. Lachele was already there waiting, too. "Did you bring your thinking cap?" she asked Gabby.

Gabby nodded. "I tried. I'm not the best at trivia, but it's fun sometimes."

"Well, I usually play cutthroat games, but if you don't think you'll be on your game, I'll just know that now and plan to have fun whether I win or lose." Dr. Lachele looked at Noah. "You know you're leading, right? We have no idea where we're going."

Noah grinned. "We're heading to the restaurant, and it's right here in the main house. It's just easier to hook up outside the restaurant because it gets so crowded on trivia night." He led them to a doorway and waved at a girl sitting at a table alone. "Come meet Paislee."

Once they were all seated, he introduced them to each other. "Paislee is my co-worker. We both love trivia, so we tend to hook up on Thursday nights and try to build a team."

"It's nice to meet you, Paislee," Gabby said softly. She wasn't sure how she felt about the other woman. Did 'hook up' mean what it seemed to mean to the girls in her dorm?

Dr. Lachele laughed. "She's lying to you, Paislee. She doesn't mind meeting you, but she's trying to figure out if you and Noah have something going because she thinks he's kind of cute."

Noah grinned at Gabby, raising an eyebrow. "You think I'm cute?"

Gabby wasn't sure what to say to that. "I don't know . . . what makes you think that's what I'm thinking?" she asked Dr. Lachele.

"Oh, didn't I mention earlier that I'm a professional matchmaker? I see a couple together, and I know right away if they'll make it or not. I have a company that introduces people at the altar." Dr. Lachele smiled at the waitress who had stopped by their table. "I'll take a Shirley Temple please. Extra cherries!"

"Just water," Gabby said, feeling very conspicuous. She had been wondering about Paislee, but the way Dr. Lachele had just blurted it out was very embarrassing for her.

After the drink orders were finished, Paislee looked over at Gabby. "I'm not sure what you're thinking or anything, but I'm just going to come right out and tell you that Noah and I are just friends and co-workers. Kissing him would be like kissing my brother and *very* disgusting."

Gabby laughed. "I hope he wasn't harboring a secret crush on you. That would have devastated him." After Paislee's words, Gabby was sure she would really like her . . . maybe even be friends with her. It was strange how one little statement made people feel better.

Noah laughed. "I feel the same way about Paislee as she feels about me. I love her like a sister, but more than that . . . no!"

"I see," Gabby said. She wasn't sure what else to say to the conversation. Should she volunteer that she was not seeing anyone?

Dr. Lachele grinned at Gabby. "Let's go in a circle. I'll start. I'm Dr. Lachele, I'm married to Sam, and I'm happy."

Dr. Lachele nodded at Paislee. "I'm Paislee. Not currently seeing anyone, and I'm happy to be playing trivia."

Noah rubbed the back of his neck, obviously a little embarrassed. "I'm Noah, not seeing anyone, and I'm happy that I get free pizza tonight."

Gabby laughed. "I'm Gabby. I'm not seeing anyone. I'm happy that I finished the book before supper, and I loved it!"

Noah looked at her in surprise. "You're a fast reader."

"I took a speed reading course in college. I needed to be able to be fast for my classes." Gabby thanked the waitress when she set her water on the table.

After all the drinks were delivered, the waitress looked at Noah. "Kelsi tells me that whatever you get tonight is on the house. Please don't break my back making me carry it all to the table!"

Gabby grinned at the woman whose nametag read, "Lucy." "You must know Noah."

"We all know Noah. No one can eat as much as he can." Lucy looked at Noah, her pencil poised over her notepad. "I think I'm ready."

He ordered chicken wings, cheese sticks, and three large pizzas for the table. The only person who looked even a little surprised was Dr. Lachele.

"Is that all?" Lucy asked.

"For now. I'm sure I'll order more later." Noah saluted her with his root beer as she hurried off to put in their order.

Gabby found she enjoyed their foursome a great deal. While they didn't win trivia, they did have a lot of fun playing, and she got to know the others better.

Toward the end of the night, a tall blonde ran over to the table and tapped Dr. Lachele on the shoulder. "I find myself in need of a boobie bump!"

Dr. Lachele stood up and spread her arms wide. "Kaya! I heard you moved to the back of beyond!"

Gabby turned to Noah. "Is that the girl who wrote the book?"

"Yup."

"She seems so . . . normal." Gabby had expected someone a bit older, with thick glasses. She wasn't sure why because she knew she'd met the woman's twin earlier that day. It was just the impression she had of her.

"Kaya's as normal as they come. She's really nice, and she prefers Belle over Cinderella," Paislee told her in a whisper.

"How do you know?" Gabby asked. "Does she run around asking everyone who her favorite princess is, too?"

"No, that's just Bridget, but Bridget picks fights with Kaya in public, demanding that her sister admit Cinderella is best."

Gabby shook her head. "Bridget seems like a character."

Kaya looked down at Gabby. "Bridget is definitely a character. I've killed her in three books now!"

Gabby laughed out loud at that. "Are you allowed to kill your sister in books?"

"As long as she doesn't know it's her, who does it hurt?" Kaya asked, winking.

"I read *Mail Order Miracle* today. I loved it. I'm trying out for the part of Frankie."

Kaya's face lit up when her book was mentioned. "I like you for Frankie. I think you have that certain something Frankie needs. You seem like a real person and not someone who expects to be served by everyone around her." She looked over at a table across the room where Sierra was holding court with several men. "She's not the right person to play Frankie for sure."

Gabby smiled. "Do you have any say in casting?"

Kaya shook her head adamantly. "None whatsoever. I get some say over the scripts, but nothing about casting. If I did have a say, I'd tell them to choose you." She looked around her. "Oh, there's Steven! He's one of the producers. Have you met him yet?"

Before Gabby knew what was going to happen, Kaya had hurried over to the producer and brought him to her table. Gabby choked on her water and knew her face was turning red. Way to make a good impression! "I'm Gabriella Tanner."

Steven nodded to her. "I'm looking forward to your audition on Saturday. I've seen your screen tests, and they were good, but I want to see both you and Sierra do the same scene."

"Do you know which scene yet?" Gabby had the script, but she didn't want to have to memorize the entire thing before Saturday. She wanted to get out and see more of the ranch.

"They didn't tell you that? Your agent was supposed to send you a letter with that information today."

"Oops. I got a letter about an hour before supper, but I wanted to finish reading *Mail Order Miracle,* and I never opened it. I'll read it when I get back to the room and start working on the script."

Steven laughed. "Just be familiar with it. We don't have to be completely off-script for the audition. Just be close, and you'll do fine." He looked over at Kaya. "Do you want to be there for the auditions? They're at ten."

Kaya groaned. "I never get up before noon." She rubbed the back of her neck. "Fine, I'll be there, but I won't be happy about it."

Steven patted her hand. "Michelle's going to be there with me. She said you were always a favorite patient of hers."

"Oh, will she meet me in the office?"

"I'm not sure how her replacement would feel about that . . ."

"I guess I shouldn't ask. I see the new guy." Kaya shrugged. "I just got really used to Dr. Michelle, and she's my friend!"

"I know. I'll see you Saturday." He nodded at Gabby before disappearing back to the table where he had been sitting with a tall, beautiful redhead.

Gabby was a bit stunned after meeting him. He was one of the directors of her favorite show, and it was strange to just meet him as an actual person and not as a director. She was looking more forward to the auditions by the moment.

She felt someone's eyes on her, and she glanced over, seeing that Sierra was staring at her across the room. Her eyes seemed to be telling Gabby that she wasn't even competition, but Gabby didn't mind. This was a good experience for her, coming to this ranch and spending time with new people, even if she didn't get the part. But oh, how she wanted it.

Noah got three desserts for himself and started eating them. Gabby yawned, stretching. "I'm still on Central time. I think I need to get to bed."

Noah shook his head. "Let me finish my desserts, and I'll walk you to your room." He couldn't just walk away from three free desserts, but he definitely wanted to spend a little more time together. She hadn't denied it when Dr. Lachele had said she thought he was cute. Maybe she'd go out with him while she was there.

Gabby nodded. "Okay, but hurry. My eyelids are starting to close. I caught my flight at five."

"Did you fly out of New Orleans?" he asked.

"Yeah, it's the nearest airport to Slidell."

"Slidell?" Dr. Lachelle asked. "I matched a girl in Louisiana a couple of years ago. Super sweet and a major Disney fan. She was a principal of a school if I remember correctly. Michelle something . . ."

"I don't know any principals who are named Michelle," Gabby said. She only knew one principal, and that was her mother's boss, and his name definitely wasn't Michelle.

"Okay. Well, I think I'm headed to see Sam. I might need to wipe away his tears if his team lost." Dr. Lachele got up then and left the table, leaving the others staring after her.

"She's an odd woman, but I think I like her," Gabby told the others.

Paislee nodded. "I concur. Very odd, but likable. We need to introduce her to Jaclyn. Can you imagine the two of them discussing matchmaking?"

Noah shrugged. "Are she and the fairies talking again? I haven't heard."

"No idea. I avoid her and the fairies as much as I can."

"Don't we all?" Noah asked.

"Okay, who is Jaclyn?" Gabby asked, looking back and forth between the other two.

"Oh, you have to meet Jaclyn!" Paislee said, her eyes bright. "She's our resident matchmaker. She's old . . . no one knows for sure how old, I don't think. She has a lawn full of garden gnomes, fairies, and leprechauns, and the fairies tell her who needs to be matched up together. But the fairies and gnomes fight a lot, and right now the fairies and Jaclyn aren't speaking, which makes things interesting. Go down toward the RV park and the lake. I promise, you will *not* miss her house."

"She lives here on the ranch?"

"Yes! She was Kelsi's grandmother's best friend," Noah said. "She's a permanent part of the landscape."

"Maybe I'll go talk to her. She seems interesting."

"If you do, let me know if she has snickerdoodles and tea hot waiting," Noah said.

"Why?" Gabby asked. That didn't make sense to her.

"Because if she does, it means the fairies told her, and they're talking again. If she doesn't, we'll know they're still at odds with each other."

Gabby decided more questions would only confuse her more. "All right."

Noah pushed his last dessert plate away, not a crumb left on the plate. "May I walk you to your room, Gabby?"

Gabby nodded. "I'd like that." Never in her life had she been as attracted to a man as she was to Noah. This may be her last chance to see him. She hoped not, but it was a definite possibility.

"Night, Paislee." Noah waved and took Gabby's hand, weaving through the tables. "Did you have fun?"

Gabby nodded. "I did. I probably need to spend tomorrow getting ready for my audition, but today was really nice. I loved the book, and I enjoyed going through the Old West Town. This ranch really is amazing."

"It is. I wish I could help you practice tomorrow, but I have to work. I'm off Saturday, and I would love to get together in the afternoon. Maybe I can help take your mind off your audition."

"I'd like that." Gabby was very excited at the prospect. She really did want to get to know him better.

"We could go snowmobiling!"

"That sounds fun, but we can't go into the mountains."

He sighed. "I won't take you anywhere that scares you." It would ruin a little of the fun for him, but maybe he could help her get used to heights little by little. He sure hoped she got the part so he'd have the opportunity.

She stopped outside her door. "This is me."

"Thanks for spending the day with me, Gabby. I really did have a very nice time."

"Thanks for going with me. I'm sure it wouldn't have been half as fun without you."

Noah leaned down and wrapped one arm around her, his hand settling under her long hair at the nape of her neck. She felt tingles run through her as he touched her there so softly. "Goodnight, Gabby."

He pressed his lips softly to hers and smiled down at her. "See you Saturday." And then he was gone.

Gabby stood staring after him. It hadn't been her first kiss, but it was her first kiss that wasn't part of a play. She'd never forget that moment with Noah, his blond hair falling over his forehead. He was a special man, and she was definitely in over her head.

Chapter Four

Gabby spent the next morning working on her lines for the scene she'd be doing the following day. She had no idea who she'd be acting with, but it would be interesting for her no matter what. Whoever it was would be up for the role of Frankie's brother Willard. She was already starting to think of the role of Frankie as hers, and she knew that was a big mistake. She was up against Sierra Barker, and in star power alone, she was greatly out-womanned.

After she finished, she glanced at her watch, realizing it was lunchtime, and she hadn't taken the time for breakfast. With a quick apology to her stomach, she pulled on her warm clothing and took the elevator to the first floor. She would walk over to the diner and enjoy watching the crazy cast of characters there on the ranch. Gabby thought they could do a sitcom based on the people there now instead of a period drama on the history of the place. Maybe she should suggest to Kaya that someone should write a romance series about the ranch. With so many babies on the way, she was sure they'd have plenty of material.

As she walked, she breathed in the cold air, realizing that she liked the dry cold of Idaho better than she liked the wet heat of Louisiana. Maybe this was a place she could get used to being—she'd have to if she got the part.

When she reached the diner, Kelsi showed her to a table, and she ordered the special and a glass of water. She'd learned a lot from Noah the day before, and part of what she'd learned was that she should order whatever Bob had on special with no question at all.

While she waited, she looked around the café, noting that the sheriff was at the next table over again. He only stayed for a few more minutes before he got up and left, leaving Gabby as the only customer.

Then a young, reasonably attractive man came into the café, and he headed straight for Kelsi, who looked both shocked and disgusted to see him there. "Hi, baby. I missed you! Why didn't you call?"

Kelsi stared at him for a moment, blinking at him. "I told you when you left I wanted nothing more to do with you. What are you doing back here? I thought you were going to play Prince Charming or someone at Disneyland."

The man sat in one of the stools in front of the bar and shrugged. "I tried to get them to see how fabulous I was, but they never let me do more than sell ice cream to tourists. Obviously, they don't recognize pure talent when they see it. I even did voices while I was selling ice cream!" He fiddled with the napkin holder in front of him while he talked. "Then I heard that you guys were going to be filming a television show here about the history of the ranch. I had to come back! I missed my girl, and I missed Idaho so much!"

"You did?" Kelsi folded her arms across her chest, obviously not willing to be part of the discussion.

"I did. So what are you doing tonight, baby?"

Kelsi blinked a couple of times before responding. "Well, after I pick my twins up from the child care facility that's now part of the ranch, I'll go home and fix supper for my husband and me. The babies will eat a little, but mostly they'll probably just throw peas onto the floor because that's what one-year-olds do."

The man was obviously taken aback. From where she was sitting, Gabby could only see his profile, but he was not pleased with Kelsi's response. "I barely left, and you married someone else? And had kids?"

Kelsi shook her head. "Donn, you left two years ago. We weren't all that close when you left. I was married shortly after that and had my twins. Two girls who are absolutely beautiful, by the way!"

Donn should his head. "I was going to come back here and sweep you off your feet. I figured if I gave you a ring, you'd marry me and maybe put in a good word for me with the producers."

"A ring?" Kelsi held up her left hand. "Notice, there's an engagement ring *and* a wedding ring. And stretch marks. Did you know that when a woman has babies they cause her stomach to grow and stretch? That's right. I'm not giving up my husband and children for anything!"

"So, who did you marry? Some guest you talked into staying?"

"No, I married the sheriff. You remember Shane Clapper." Kelsi smiled then as she saw her husband walk through the door standing behind Donn. "I love him with everything inside me. I never gave *you* a second thought."

"You married the sheriff?" Donn sounded disgusted. "How could you marry that loser? I'm going to be a star, and instead, you choose some small-town sheriff who probably doesn't know his gun from his man-beater-stick."

"You don't think he does? Maybe you'd like a demonstration . . ." Shane's voice was low, but Donn heard him. He spun around and glared at him.

"You moved in on my girl as soon as I left town!" Donn said.

"You bet I did. I went out with her that night and was married less than two weeks later. I hope you're enjoying working for that giant rodent out in California . . ." Shane walked around the counter and kissed Kelsi. "I'm taking off a couple of hours early tonight so I can cook supper. I'll pick the girls up, too! You just put your feet up when you get home."

Kelsi grinned. "That sounds lovely! All we need is a sitter for some quality time."

Gabby had made no secret of the fact she was watching the entire conversation. "I'll watch the twins. I'm good with babies."

Kelsi bit her lip. "I really appreciate the offer, but the Kids' Korral is twenty-four hours per day. They're used to the place. Let's just leave them a little late tonight."

Shane nodded. "Sounds wonderful." He put his hand over Kelsi's tummy that Gabby hadn't noticed before. She was always wearing bulky clothes, but the gesture made her realize something. "Take care of my son . . ."

Donn glared at Kelsi as Shane left again. "You're knocked up again?"

"I prefer to think of it as carrying another special little person. If you don't plan to order food, then get out, Donn. I will not recommend you for the show." She walked toward the kitchen and picked up the plate waiting there. "I have work to do."

Donn left, but the angry look on his face worried Gabby a little. "He doesn't look pleased."

Kelsi shook her head, sitting down in the booth across from Gabby. "He's worthless. I dated him for like five years because I just didn't care enough either way to break it off. As soon as he left, Shane and I got married. Shane is the love of my life, and Donn is wasted time." She put her feet up beside Gabby. "And we haven't told anyone we're expecting yet, but Shane couldn't help but throw it in Donn's face. Now everyone on the ranch is going to know in about thirty minutes." Kelsi rubbed the back of her neck. "I think I'm going for a massage soon. I'm tired and cranky, and that man makes me crazy."

Gabby grinned at her before taking a big bite of her gumbo. "Bob can cook!"

"He knows it, too," Kelsi said smiling. "We're almost ready to close for the day. You finish your lunch, but I'm going to lock up. I don't want any more customers or ex-boyfriends wandering in here as if I want them around."

Gabby grinned. "I'll hurry."

"Nah, take your time. I'm just explaining why I'm locking the door. We close at two, and I'm ready. Date night with Shane. It's time!" Kelsi hurried over and locked the door, carrying all the salt and pepper shakers over to Gabby's table. "I'm going to sit with you while I work. Gabbing with Gabby will help the time go by faster."

Gabby laughed as expected. "Maybe someday I'll have my own talk show. 'Gabbing with Gabby.' What do you think?"

"As long as you play Frankie for about ten years first, I think that's a great idea."

"Oh, do you think the show will go that long? I'm excited to have the final audition tomorrow. Well, excited and nervous."

Kelsi nodded. "I can understand that. Have you always known you wanted to act?"

Gabby laughed at that. "I was an *accounting* major, and I have a scholarship waiting for me in Texas to get my MBA. I'm only here because I was in a play at school and somehow the producers of *Legacy* got their hands on the tape of the show. They specifically asked me to audition. I feel way over my head here!"

"Wow. I can understand that. I would, too. I'm sure you'll do great, though. They wouldn't have asked you to audition unless they felt strongly that you were the right person for the part." Kelsi poured salt into the shaker in front of her. "I can't see Sierra in that part at all. She's more the type to play a debutante than someone who wears men's clothes in a time that pants were only for men."

"The two scenes for the audition show both sides of Frankie. I'll have to be a debutante in a ball gown, hating every minute of it, and then I'll have to be standing looking out over the land with Willard. I already think of Frankie as mine. I know I shouldn't be so excited about the part before I get it, but I can feel it's meant to be mine!"

"I think so!" Kelsi grinned. "I wish I had a say in who they were casting because I'd tell them to have Sierra go home. You are just right for the part, and why I know that I don't know." She sighed. "What do you think of the name Widget for a little boy?"

"Widget?" Gabby was certain Kelsi must have lost her mind. "That's not a real name, is it?"

"Well, no, not yet, but I really think it should be! Don't you?"

"Not particularly. What does Shane think of it?"

"Oh, Shane just mumbles things like, 'Over my dead body,' and 'Kelsi, we're not naming a child Widget.' He has no taste in names!"

Gabby finished as much of her gumbo as she could eat before pushing the bowl away. "I have to side with Shane on this one, Kelsi. I'm sorry. I'm all for female solidarity, but not when it comes to naming a child Widget!"

Kelsi studied Gabby for a moment. "Have you ever had a child?"

"No."

"Well, then I want you to imagine carrying a baby for nine months. A baby that kicks, rolls over, and plays the drum solo from 'Wipe Out' on your ribs! Then tell me you don't get to be creative with the name attached to that little human!"

Gabby leaned forward. "Creative is one thing. Cruel is something else entirely."

Kelsi made a face. "Want me to put the meal on your room?"

"Yes, please. I'm heading out. I want to work a little more on my lines for the audition tomorrow, and there's someone I want to meet," Gabby said, sliding out of the booth.

"Who do you want to meet?" Kelsi asked.

"Someone named Jaclyn. I was told where to find her and what her house looks like. She sounds very special."

Kelsi grinned. "Jaclyn is very special. Do you feel like you're being nudged to talk to her?"

"I sort of do. They talked about her at trivia last night, and I just knew I had to meet her." Gabby looked at Kelsi suspiciously. "Why does that amuse you?"

"I just have a feeling I know where this is going. . . . Enjoy your day, and tell Jaclyn I said, 'Hi!'"

"Will do." Gabby left the restaurant feeling a little confused, but she wasn't sure why. Kelsi obviously knew something about Jaclyn she didn't.

As she walked, she admired the ranch, covered in snow as it was. She knew she was meeting the director in the Old West Town the next morning for the audition, and she hoped it went well. Every minute she spent in this marvelous place made her want the part even more—so she would *never* have to leave.

When she reached the house with gnomes, fairies, and leprechauns surrounding it, she went to the door and knocked. The woman that came to the door seemed a bit odd to her. She opened the door wide, and Gabby saw bunnies hopping everywhere. "I'm sorry I don't have tea and snickerdoodles ready for you. The fairies and I are no longer on speaking terms, and they're not telling me when I'm getting guests. Sit! Sit! I'll get some cookies and tea for you anyway!" The older woman hurried into the kitchen and put tea on the stove. "Are you here for the show?"

Gabby called back, "I'm here to audition for Frankie."

Jaclyn clapped her hands together. "Oh, that's wonderful. We need a good Frankie to carry the show." She waved her hand. "Just move one of the bunnies off the couch. They know they're supposed to get down when I have guests anyway."

Gabby pushed a bunny aside, and sat down, feeling like she'd just done something evil. She wanted to take all of the rabbits home with her. They were so fluffy! "I'm sorry to drop in unannounced this way. I just wanted to meet you."

"Are you looking for matchmaking help? The gnomes are trying to help me, but they're not nearly as adept at it as the fairies, and as I said, the fairies still won't talk to me. Dratted creatures think they're better than everyone else in the mythological world. Well, let me tell you something, little actress girl whose name the gnomes don't know . . . they're not better than anyone!"

Jaclyn walked back into the room with a teapot on a tray. There were also cookies and three teacups. "Three cups?" Gabby asked. "I'm Gabby, by the way."

"I don't find you overly talkative." The older woman threw her head back and laughed hysterically at her own joke. "Sorry about that. I couldn't resist. Gorgeous George says someone else is headed this way."

"Is Gorgeous George one of your bunnies?" Gabby asked, ignoring the joke about her name.

"The bunnies don't talk! Are you daft, girl? No, Gorgeous George is one of the gnomes. He's standing outside, and he can see people coming." Jaclyn jumped up at a knock on the door.

Gabby was disappointed. She'd wanted to visit with Jaclyn by herself, but when she saw it was Dr. Lachele, she grinned. She had a feeling the two matchmakers would get along famously.

"Come in and sit down," Jaclyn told Dr. Lachele. "You'll have to move a bunny, but it's not a problem." She poured tea into three cups and handed one to each of her guests. "Now, who're you? I love the purple hair, by the way. Do you think I could pull off purple hair?"

Gabby choked on her tea, trying to imagine the old gray-haired woman with purple hair.

Dr. Lachele nodded. "I think everyone would look better with purple hair, but there wouldn't be as much variety in the world which would be a shame." She took a sip of her tea. "I hear you're the resident matchmaker. I'm a matchmaker, too. I introduce people at the altar."

"Really?" Jaclyn asked, looking excited. "I match people with the help of fairies . . . or I did before they stopped speaking to me." She looked over at Gabby. "I can do a little on my own . . . for instance, I think this young lady should go to either Andrew or Noah."

"Noah," Lachele said without hesitation. "I played trivia with them last night, and it didn't take any time at all to see that the two of them belong together. I don't know who Andrew is, but she belongs with Noah."

Gabby sank back into the cushions on the couch, wondering if the two of them could possibly be right. Was she meant for Noah?

Chapter Five

Gabby barely heard more of the conversation as the two women discussed why Noah was the perfect man for her. She hadn't flown to Idaho looking for love. She really hadn't expected anything, and now look at her . . . she'd had her first real kiss, and two matchmakers were talking about how she belonged with the man who had kissed her.

But could she make it work with him? He seemed like a daredevil to her. Would she freak out every time she knew he was going up onto the mountain? She hoped not, but she really wasn't sure one way or the other.

When she zeroed in on the conversation again, she realized the two matchmakers were no longer talking about her and instead were talking about how to tell if a couple was right for each other. Dr. Lachele said she didn't even have to see people together to know if they'd be right. It was just an overwhelming feeling which two people should be together, and she'd never had a marriage fail in all her years as a matchmaker.

Gabby listened for as long as she could, but the conversation was really a bit too much for her, considering they'd begun it with her and Noah. She got to her feet. "Thank you for the tea and cookies, Jaclyn."

Jaclyn grinned, the look almost evil. "Conversation too much for you, Gabby?"

Gabby shrugged, heading for the door. "It just might be." She slipped out quietly, walking back toward the main house, where she was staying. After a moment, she stopped and turned, going back toward the lake. She wasn't sure if it would be frozen over or not, but even if it was, she hoped to find it calming.

Her heart was racing at the idea of a real relationship. Never in her life had she felt an automatic connection with a man like so many of her friends had talked about. Noah was different though, and she'd felt drawn to him in a way she never had any other man. Cooking for him would be a formidable task, but for now, she was going to enjoy his company when she could.

She went down to the shore of the lake and sat on a park bench. It wasn't covered with snow, which told her that other people had been there recently as well. She sat and looked out at the mostly frozen lake, wondering what had really brought her to Idaho. Was it some sort of fate—something she'd never believed in before—drawing her toward the man she was supposed to spend her life with? Or was she meant to play Frankie in *Legacy?* Or was it both?

After what seemed like hours, but was in reality a much shorter time, she got to her feet and walked back toward the main house. She had no plans for supper because she hadn't thought she could get her lines memorized so quickly.

When she got to the main house, she saw Noah leaning against the building, his arms folded across his chest, his right foot propped against the building, as he watched her approach. "I thought maybe you could use some help running over your lines," he called to her.

She grinned, nodding. She didn't need help. She had the lines down cold, but she loved the idea of spending the evening with him. "Sounds good. Are you hungry?" she asked.

He laughed. "Who do you think you're talking to? Do you want to go into town for supper, and then we can come back here and work on your lines?"

"I'd really like that."

He took her hand and pulled her around to the parking lot at the other side of the main house. "We had pizza last night. Want Chinese? Italian? American food? Any preference?"

She shrugged. "Doesn't really matter to me. I'll eat a tenth of what you do anyway, so you should get to choose."

"Good point! We could go to Post Falls for steak, if that sounds good!"

"You decide. I'm really just along for the ride."

"How long will it take you to go over all your lines?" he asked.

"It'll take about twenty minutes. I've got them memorized, but I'd love to have someone go over them with me again to make sure I have them down cold."

Noah opened the passenger door on a pick-up truck for her, and she climbed up into the vehicle. She was a relatively tall woman, but the truck was still higher than she would have liked. She had to grab the handle and figure out how to maneuver herself in. There was a step, but it really wasn't much help!

He turned some music on low, so they could talk to each other. "I'm in the mood for steak. Do you mind an hour drive round trip?"

"Not at all. It really won't take us long to get me where I need to be for my audition tomorrow. Can I tell you something crazy?"

"Sure! I love crazy." Noah watched the road as they talked, knowing this windy road they were taking through the mountains would make her nervous.

"When I came here yesterday, I wasn't sure if I even wanted the part. Now that I've read the book the show is based on, seen this place, and met some of the people, I know I *need* to be Frankie. Frankie is me, and I am Frankie."

He grinned at that. "Not crazy at all. I took one look at you and knew you were meant to be mine."

She blinked a few times, wondering what had led to him saying that. "Have you been talking to Jaclyn or Dr. Lachele?"

He laughed. "No, but it wouldn't surprise me if they were saying the same thing. Were they?"

"They were, but it was so weird! I wasn't expecting it at all!" Gabby crossed her arms over her chest, staring straight ahead. Should she even be discussing this with him?

"Well, I'm not going to get down on one knee and propose because Jaclyn and Dr. Lachele think I should, but I sure do want to get to know you better. You're already pretty special to me, and not just because I got to eat free for an entire day because you were with me!"

She laughed. "Well, I'm glad you're not just in it for the free food. With the way you are, it's hard to tell at times."

"I can understand that. My mother used to tell me that if I was offered endless riches or an all-you-can-eat feast, I'd have a hard time choosing which I wanted." Noah shrugged. "Just goes to prove she knows me well! At that time, I'd have picked the feast. Now I'd take the money because I know I could buy many endless feasts."

"The day a woman is as important to you as food, you'll know you've found the right one."

He nodded. "I do believe that to be true."

A short while later, they pulled into a parking lot, and he got out and walked around to open her door for her. Taking her hand, he walked with her to the front of the restaurant. "They have dancing here and really good steak. I think it's worth the drive."

"I'm more than willing to try it out."

Once they were seated with their menus, he asked, "How nervous are you about tomorrow?"

"I'm nervous and excited all at once. I hate the idea of being a big star . . . I don't want my name on people's lips . . . but I love the idea of playing this part and staying at River's End."

"Any idea who the male lead will be?"

She shook her head. "No, they're starting the story before the book starts. So their decision to go west is there and their first years on the ranch. Wally won't be in the story until three or four seasons in, from what I understand. Assuming the show goes that long, of course."

"Interesting. So your hero, at least in the beginning, will be your brother!"

"Yup. And I have heard no rumors at all about who they're looking at to play my brother." She laughed and shook her head. "Look at me talking like the part is mine. I'm up against *Sierra Barker.* How could I even make an assumption like that?"

"Because Sierra is wrong for the part. I think everyone knows that. They need someone with a fresh face and a sweet attitude, and that's you. Sierra would make the rest of the cast crazy in a week. She's one of those actresses that is known for making everyone she works with angry."

"But she's a great deal more experienced than me, which means she's got the star power to bring people into the show who wouldn't normally watch it."

"Yes, she does. But I'm betting money you wouldn't cost as much, and you fit the part better." He looked up from his menu at her for a moment. "Besides, I want you to stay."

She smiled at that, not sure if she was flattered or a bit frightened. Frightened seemed to fit better. She didn't know why anything different in life frightened her so much, but it did. It had been all she could do to get on a plane to Idaho. "Hopefully the director will say the same thing tomorrow."

"Steven will be at the audition, too, won't he?" Noah asked, finally setting his menu down.

"Yes, I think so . . . why?"

"I was part of the rescue team who helped get him down the mountain. I don't usually help search and rescue, but Dani saw me, and she asked. . . ."

Gabby felt the fear rising within her at the thought of having to be rescued from the mountain. "What happened to him?"

Noah shook his head. "He actually *did* fall off the mountain. Do you believe?"

"Yes! Those mountains look terrifying! You told me only stupid people fell off the mountain, and Steven Pickman is anything but stupid!"

Noah's eyes widened as he realized he'd triggered her fear. "You're not going to fall off the mountain. I would never let that happen to you. He was there alone, and you won't be. I'll be with you every step of the way."

"They'd better not want me to climb that mountain for the audition tomorrow. Maybe I'll eventually be able to, but not this month, and certainly not tomorrow."

He covered her hand with his. "I'm sorry, Gabby. I shouldn't have mentioned that. It was a freak accident."

"Freak accidents are scary! That's why they're freak . . . which is short for freaky!"

"I won't let it happen to you, okay? Don't go up the mountain without me."

Gabby worked on slowing her breathing. "So if I trust you, I can't be scared. Is that what you're saying?"

"Not at all. I'm just saying that you'll always have me to lean on. And if you get scared, I'll be beside you or wherever you need me to be. Even if it's in front of you so you don't have to see how far down it is."

She smiled at that. "You're a nice man, Noah . . . why don't I know your last name?"

He shrugged. "Do you need to know it? What if it's a last name that's just dreadful! Like Humperdink?"

"What does it matter? What's your last name, Noah?"

"It's Andrews. Just don't use the information against me!"

She shook her head at him. "And how could I do that?"

"No idea. Just don't, okay?"

"I won't." Gabby looked over as their waitress came to take their order. As usual, Noah ordered two meals, and she got a small one. After the waitress walked away, she frowned. "Should I have gotten a bigger meal so you could finish it?"

He shrugged. "I can live with just two meals. I might waste away to nothing, but I can do it. I'll be brave!"

She shook her head at him. "You'll have to eat six desserts to make up for it."

"We'll stop and get six packages of Oreos on our way back to the ranch." He took a piece of bread from the center of the table and buttered it. "And they'll refill this if I want them to." He eyed her suspiciously. "Are you going to have some of my bread?"

"I couldn't do that to you! No, all the bread is yours."

"You're good to me." He leaned back in the booth, taking a big bite of the bread and chewing it before saying, "Tell me what your scenes will be like tomorrow."

"There are two. The first will be Frankie and Willard back east discussing their need to get away from the balls and the affluence of their lives. They want to do something meaningful."

"Sounds fun. What will you wear for that?" he asked.

"I doubt they'll have me in costume for the audition, but for the show, I'd be in a formal dress. Hoop skirt and all." She shuddered a little. "I'm more like Frankie than I care to admit. Dresses are only acceptable when absolutely necessary."

"I got the impression that by the time Wally got to the ranch she wanted to wear dresses again."

"True . . .but that part of the show will be years down the road, if it comes at all. This first part is just Willard and Frankie trying to make their way in the Idaho wilderness on a claim no one else wanted because it was too mountainous." She took a sip of her water, watching him. Never had she felt as comfortable with a man as she did with Noah, and it was nice to just spend time with him. "The second scene will be Frankie and Willard looking over the land they've chosen. I think both scenes are from the first two-hour pilot episode. I've read over the whole script, and I think it's a really good introduction to the characters and their struggles."

"I wonder if they'll stray from family history and let Willard live long enough to marry and have kids. That part made me sad after I read the book. I wanted Willard to fall in love and marry, too, but he died too young."

Gabby frowned. "I didn't know that."

"Yeah, it was part of what Pastor Kevin dug up when he researched the family."

"Well, the show is a fictionalized version of the family's history. So is the book for that matter. Pastor Kevin said that Frankie really did send for a mail-order husband, but not a lot is known about Wally." She wished she could travel back in time and meet the first settlers of the ranch. She already felt so connected to the place and the people who lived there. "Maybe they'll let Willard live to be a ripe old age."

"But then why would Frankie's children inherit? That's the question. How would they make that work out?"

"No idea. I'm not a screenwriter. I'm more of a numbers girl."

Noah shook his head. "Don't even say *that* again. I cannot imagine you spending the rest of your life working with numbers. You need to be on television, showing the whole world how good you are."

She frowned at that. "What makes you think I'm good? You've never seen me act!"

"That's true! Why haven't you acted for me yet? You're acting for the directors tomorrow, and I feel like you're giving them a part of yourself you haven't given me yet!" Noah put one wrist against his forehead. "Oh, woe is me!"

She rolled her eyes. "You'll see me act tonight when we go over my lines together. I sure hope I have a chance against Sierra. She makes me so nervous."

"Do you really think they'd waste time and money flying you both here for a final audition if you didn't have a real chance? I spent some time with Steven, and I promise you, he's not a man to waste money where his projects are concerned."

Their plates were brought then, and Noah attacked his food with a vengeance. Gabby shook her head, knowing then that if their relationship went anywhere, she'd always come after his food.

After they'd eaten, they headed back to the ranch, and Noah really did pull in somewhere for several packages of Oreos. "I'm sorry, but I have to have more to eat than that!"

"You had two twenty-two-ounce steaks."

"Yeah? So?"

Gabby grinned at him, shaking her head. She hadn't been able to finish her six-ounce steak, and he'd finished it for her, which had not surprised her even a little bit.

Back at the main house, he went up to her room with her, and she gave him the script, telling him what page the first scene was on. He read Willard's lines, and she read Frankie's, feeling so much like she was going to play the heroine.

When they were done, he turned to the next scene. She got every single word right, and her passion for the story was obvious to him. "You're going to kill it tomorrow, Gabby. Stop worrying. If the part is not yours, I'll go on a diet for a week!"

She laughed. "You really believe in me if you're willing to bet that!"

He caught her hand and pulled her down next to him on the bed, cupping her face in his hands. "I do believe in you. More than I've ever believed in anyone. You're awfully special to me already, Gabby."

She sighed, looking into his eyes. "Thank you, Noah. I need that."

He leaned down and brushed his lips against hers. "I wish I could be there for the audition tomorrow, but I'll be working."

"I'll see you after, and we'll go on a picnic or something."

"In the snow? Are we already turning you into an Idaho girl?"

She shrugged. "There are worse things I could be!"

Chapter Six

When Gabby woke the following morning, she immediately knew where she was and why she was there. Sometimes she wouldn't if she wasn't somewhere familiar, but she did there. She wasn't sure why. Instead of thinking about where she was sleeping, she woke up with Noah on her mind. She showered quickly before rushing downstairs. She had an hour before auditions, but Noah had told her about something at the bakery she had to try. Every Saturday morning, Miranda made kolaches, and he made them sound like the most delicious thing in the entire world. She needed to try them before going home to Louisiana. She knew she'd go back if only to pack her clothes for her move to Idaho. Already she hated the thought of leaving this beautiful place, even for a short while.

She bundled up as warmly as she could and made her way to the Old West Town. There she found the bakery, and Miranda was there, with two girls who looked to be a little younger than Gabby was. There was a long line out the door.

She shivered a little as she waited her turn, finally getting to the front door. "Please tell me you have kolaches!" She needed to at least try them.

The girl at the counter nodded. "We do! Do you want sausage and cheese or ham and cheese?"

"Ham and cheese please. I'd like two." Noah had said he usually ate six, so Gabby was sure two would be more than enough for her.

Miranda saw her and called from the back. "I can't come say hi because we're almost out of kolaches, and I need to make more, but I'll see you soon!"

Gabby lifted her bag triumphantly. "I got mine! See you later!" She left the bakery, weaving in and out of people. It was amazing how devoted these people were to Miranda's culinary creations.

She walked over to a bench in front of the general store, which appeared to be closed. She wasn't sure if it was closed for the morning or just not open yet, but it didn't matter to her a whole lot. She was there to watch the people from the show set everything up.

She wasn't surprised when she saw Steven Pickman giving his input to everything. He wanted props moved to different places and camera angles to be different. She had a lot of respect for him and his work, and she enjoyed watching him in his element.

She felt someone sit down beside her and turned her head. "Are you here to watch the auditions?"

The woman shook her head. "I'm here to support my husband, Steven. He wanted me to be here, so I am, whether I want to be or not." She turned to Gabby fully. "I'm Michelle Pickman. It still feels weird to call myself that."

Gabby grinned. "I knew he'd recently gotten married. I'm Gabriella Tanner, but everyone just calls me Gabby. I'm trying out for the lead, and I'm terribly nervous." She instantly liked this woman in front of her and knew they could be friends.

Michelle grinned. "Don't be! Steven is *not* a fan of Sierra Barker."

"Well, that certainly adds to my confidence level!" Gabby shook her head. "It's kind of intimidating to be a nobody up against someone like *Sierra Barker.*"

"A nobody? I don't think that's how any of the producers or directors see you. They want you to have this part. Sierra pulled some strings to get this third interview, and no one is exactly pleased with her."

"I'm not sure you're supposed to be telling me this . . ." Gabby certainly wasn't going to complain about the insider information, but she wasn't sure if Steven would.

"Why not? I'm giving the person my husband wants for the job more confidence. How could that possibly be a bad thing?"

"Have you read the book?" Gabby asked, wondering just how much this woman knew.

"Yes! Of course I have. I was the chiropractor here on the ranch until a couple of months ago when Steven fell off the mountain and stole my heart." Michelle shook her head. "Jaclyn went so far as to accuse him of falling off the mountain just to meet me."

"That sounds just like her! Have you met Dr. Lachele?"

"Who's Dr. Lachele? I'm Dr. Michelle!"

"Oh, that could get confusing." Gabby shook her head. "Dr. Lachele is a matchmaker who introduces people at the altar. She's here for a vacation and because she knows Kaya and Bridget, but she and Jaclyn are bonding in a way that can't possibly be good for the rest of us."

"Oh my. Two matchmakers loose on the ranch? The world may implode!"

Kaya wandered over then, squeezing between Michelle and Gabby. "Dr. Michelle, have I told you I miss you? And that I want you to leave Steven and live on the ranch full time again?"

Michelle sighed. "Do you not like the new chiropractor?"

"Oh, he's fine. He's just not you!" Kaya rested her head on Michelle's shoulder. "You need to adjust me while you're here."

Michelle just laughed, patting Kaya. "Not this visit!"

"Fine." Kaya turned her attention to Gabby. "How are you enjoying the ranch?"

"I love it! This place is absolutely amazing, and it will break my heart if I don't get the part and have to leave." Gabby saw that the set was mostly ready. "Is it time to get nervous yet?" She watched to see if anyone was motioning her over for her audition, but they didn't seem to be yet.

Kaya shook her head. "Nope, and do you know why?"

"Why?" Gabby asked.

"Because *you're Frankie.* Everyone who has met you and read the book can see it. You have this part."

Gabby started taking deep breaths. "I hope so. I want it so badly I can taste it."

Steven motioned toward Gabby, and she got to her feet, walking over to join him. She continued her deep, even breaths, hoping they'd calm her down a little.

"Nervous?" he asked.

She nodded. "Now that I've read the book, I *really* want to play Frankie."

"Show us what you've got!" Steven motioned for a man to come toward them. "This is Maynard Butts. We want to see how the two of you work together. He's one of the last two actors for Willard."

Gabby smiled and held her hand out to shake his. "It's nice to meet you. I'm Gabriella Tanner."

"Nice to meet you. Break a leg!"

"You too."

Through the first scene, where they were pretending to be in a ballroom back east, they got along well, both of them enjoying themselves immensely. Gabby was in a pair of jeans and a sweater, and she mimicked being in a crowded ballroom perfectly. She enjoyed the scene with Maynard a great deal, so glad he would be her brother and not her love interest. She couldn't imagine having to kiss the man.

When they had finished, she resumed her seat with Dr. Michelle and Kaya, pleased when Kaya was so excited about her performance. "You did so good! I can't wait to see you in the other scene!"

"Aren't you supposed to be sleeping?" Michelle asked Kaya.

"Yes, but your husband invited me to come watch, and this is my book baby, and I'm going to watch it turned into a television show. You can't stop me!"

As they all watched, Sierra was paired with Jacob Myers, and the two of them did the same scene. Gabby felt her heart flutter as she watched. The two of them weren't nearly as good as she and Maynard had been. She could feel it!

Sierra and Maynard were paired for the second scene, and they went first. Gabby didn't like the way Sierra played "her" character. It felt forced and not at all authentic.

When it was her turn with Jacob, they worked together well, but she didn't feel the same chemistry she'd felt with Maynard. Maynard felt as if he really could be her brother, but Jacob just felt like someone she was trying to act with. It was hard for her to even explain it in her own thoughts, but she knew if Jacob got the part and she did, too, she'd have to turn down the role. She couldn't work with him.

When the auditions were over, Steven gathered the four actors who had been trying out for the parts and told them all they would have an answer by the end of the day. "I know that's really fast, but we'd like to start filming in ten weeks. That means we need people in place and costumes made."

Sierra flipped her long, blond hair over her shoulder. "I'm sure there's no need to even wait, Steven. Tell this no-name that the part is mine, so she can go home in shame."

Steven shook his head. "Sierra, even if we liked you for the role, that kind of attitude is not what we're looking for. We want a cohesive family atmosphere for this group. Not someone who is rude to the others."

Sierra wrinkled her nose. "Are you telling me you're actually *considering* her?"

"Yes, I really am, or she wouldn't be here today. I think she's done a wonderful job in all of her readings so far, and we're going to all discuss the choices we have." Steven nodded. "Thank you all for coming here." With those words he turned and walked away, leaving Sierra looking furious.

Gabby turned away but stopped when there was a hand on her shoulder. "You're not going to get my part. Do you hear me?" Sierra hissed.

"I don't know why you even want it!" Gabby said. "It doesn't suit you at all. You belong in a period piece with long dresses and perfect hair. This one is going to be a girl running around in men's pants and doing manual labor."

"I'm tired of being type-cast. I'm going to get this part." Sierra turned and walked away, and Gabby just shrugged. She'd promised to meet Noah back at the main house, and she wasn't going to give up a single minute with him. The clock was already ticking down.

WHILE NOAH WAITED FOR Gabby, he made sure he'd packed the snowmobile he planned to take her on well. He would take her around the ranch and just a little way up into the mountains. He wanted her to love them as much as he did.

When she reached him, her face was a bit bewildered. He frowned at her. "Is everything all right?"

She nodded. "Sierra was kind of nasty toward me, and I'm not sure why. It's not like she considers me serious competition." The other woman had made that *very* clear.

"She should." Noah handed her a helmet. "We're going for a ride. I packed a picnic lunch."

She tilted her head to one side, considering. "Is that snowmobile strong enough to carry you, me, *and* all the food you'll eat for lunch?"

"I sure hope so!" He winked at her, fastening his own helmet on and throwing one leg over the machine. "Sit behind me and hold on tight."

"Hmm . . . is this to show me the ranch or for your own sinister pleasures?"

"Is there a difference?" Noah started the machine, and they started out slowly, increasing speed as she laughed. "Fun, isn't it?"

"I should probably be scared, but I'm not. This is a lot of fun!" As they flew over the different parts of the ranch, they passed Jaclyn's house, and she saw the woman out front, Dr. Lachele at her side. She lifted a hand in a wave, amazed at her own daring.

He took them around the perimeter of the ranch not going up at all and finally stopped the machine for a minute in an out of the way spot to turn around and look at her. "I want to take you up, just a little, to have lunch. There's a really nice picnic spot. Won't take more than fifteen minutes to get to."

Gabby eyed him for a moment, wondering if her heart could handle the excitement. Finally, she nodded. "Let's do it. You'll bring me back if I'm scared, though, right?"

He kissed her then, clunking the fronts of their helmets together, both of them laughing. "Absolutely. I won't do anything that frightens you . . . too much."

"Who gets to determine too much?"

He shrugged. "We'll decide together."

"That scares me!"

He laughed, starting the machine again and heading toward the mountain. She wrapped her arms around him and held on for dear life, realizing that he was staying as far from the edge as possible as he took them up the path.

It wasn't long before they'd reached a small plateau, and he stopped the vehicle. He got off, offering her a hand. "There's a picnic pavilion here. I can start a small fire in the pit if it's too cold for you."

She shook her head. "It's downright balmy. What is it? Twenty-seven degrees today? That's like a heatwave!"

"For a Louisiana girl, you sure are adapting well!" He unpacked the lunches he'd brought with them, and carried them to the table, spreading out a tablecloth. "I thought you'd like it to be a romantic picnic with a tablecloth and everything."

She grinned. "Very nice. I wouldn't have known you had it in you!"

He laughed at that. "Well, I try. And I asked Paislee for some advice on girls." He wasn't even ashamed of asking. She knew he was a complete loss where women were concerned, and she'd been excited to help what little she could.

"You sure you don't feel anything for her?"

He made a face. "Kissing Paislee would be like kissing a sister, only I don't have a sister, and I'd have to substitute my brother's face, and ewww!"

She realized then that she'd forgotten how high up they were. "I'm going to look and see if I freak out."

He sighed. "Can't you wait until after we eat? If you do freak out, then I have to take you down the mountain before I can eat!" His stomach needed to be appeased, fear or no fear.

"What was I thinking? Of course you need to eat first! How could I have forgotten that stomach of yours?" Gabby turned and looked toward the edge anyway, needing to know if she could handle it. "It's beautiful."

Noah moved around the table closer to her, wrapping his arms around her from behind, hoping she wouldn't get scared, and not because he was hungry. "You all right?"

She nodded. "I really think I am. I'm surprised by how all right. I don't know if it's because you're with me or because it's just so breathtaking . . . but I could do this again."

Noah smiled. "Good. Now that we've discovered you're all right, let's eat!"

She laughed. "I'm sorry. I know it's been at least an hour since your last snack."

"I did have a bag of chips and a box of raisins while I waited for you." He pulled out the boxed lunch he'd brought. "Bob made us a couple of lunches. I figured we couldn't go wrong!"

"No, we couldn't!" Gabby had just taken a bite of her sandwich when her phone rang from her pocket. "Probably my mom checking on me. She hates that I'm so far away and not checking in every two point three seconds." She dug her phone out of her pocket and looked at the screen. "I don't know this number. They couldn't have made a decision already, could they?" Giving Noah a half-frightened look, she answered. "Hello?"

"Gabby? This is Steven Pickman. Are you busy?" His voice was brisk and businesslike.

"Having lunch on the mountain," she said with a smile. Her heart was beating faster, and her hands were clammy despite the cold.

"That sounds lovely. I've done that with my beautiful bride a time or two. I wanted to call you and let you know that we've made our decision."

Gabby closed her eyes. With the way he'd worded it, she knew that Sierra had gotten the part. "Thanks for letting me audition," she said softly. "And I've loved every moment here at the ranch."

"And you'll continue loving the ranch because you're playing Frankie. I'd love to talk contracts with you later this afternoon. How long will you be picnicking on the mountain, do you think?"

She looked over at Noah, her eyes giving him the answer he wanted. "How long before we go back?"

Noah looked at the time on his own phone. "I can have you back by two."

"Would two o' clock work?"

"Absolutely. I'll see you at the main house then. Meet me in the lobby. We've been given use of an office for our meeting."

"Thank you. Who's playing Willard?" she asked. She needed it to be Maynard.

"Maynard Butts. You two have a feel together on camera that made us all believe you were brother and sister."

"Wonderful. I'll talk to you soon then."

"Stay safe coming down!" Steven responded, ending the call.

Gabby sat quietly for a moment, forcing herself to breathe. Then she let out a scream loud enough to be heard down at the ranch. "I got the part!"

Noah felt as if a weight had lifted off his chest. "So you're staying?"

"Well, I'll need to go home and pack my things, and I'm not sure when I'm supposed to be here, but I have to assume I'll be here soon on a more permanent basis." She closed her eyes for a moment, trying to let it all sink in. "I'm not going to make something up, though I'd like to. I'll have more information after I've signed the contract at two."

"I'm going to wait in the lobby for you, so I can hear all the details." Noah shook his head. "No, I'm not. I'm going to get dressed up, and I'm going to take you out to celebrate tonight." He took a huge bite of his sandwich. "Do you want to go to the restaurant here at the ranch? Or somewhere a little quieter in town?"

"In town sounds really good to me. I'm not sure I want to share the moment with anyone but you." She reached out and took his hand. "I'm so glad you were with me when I found out. Now I probably really should call my mother."

He frowned. "Aren't you going to finish your lunch?"

"I couldn't eat a thing!"

He shrugged and reached over, picking up her sandwich. If she couldn't eat it, he sure could. There was never a reason to let good food go to waste.

Chapter Seven

Noah dropped her off in front of the main house at two, heading off to change for their dinner date. It wasn't time to eat yet, but he'd find a snack in the meantime, and he'd quietly celebrate the fact that Gabby would be spending more time on the ranch . . . with him.

After giving Noah her helmet, she smoothed down her hair and walked sedately into the main house. She wanted to run, skip, and jump, but she didn't want to be seen as childish in front of her new employer either.

When she got to the lobby, she was surprised by what she saw. Sierra was there, her arms flying in every direction. Gabby caught the words, "You gave a nobody the part over me?"

Steven caught Gabby's eye and motioned her forward. "Yes, I did. Gabby fits the part, and you don't."

Sierra glared at Gabby. "I've never even heard of you."

Gabby shrugged. "That's okay. It won't hurt me when I'm acting at all." She refused to back down to the viper. She'd heard too many stories of the way the diva treated women in Hollywood.

Steven laughed softly. "I have an empty office ready to go over your contract with you." He nodded to Sierra. "I hope you have better luck with the next part you go after." Then he led Gabby from the room, refusing to listen to the seasoned actress as she shouted behind them.

Gabby still couldn't believe this was really happening. She'd half-expected him to tell her he was joking when she'd come back to the main house to meet with him. "Thank you for considering a 'nobody' like me when the part came available."

Steven shook his head. "Someone needs to duct tape that woman's mouth shut and leave her that way for a year or six."

"Oh, I know no one's ever heard of me. I figured it would always be that way." She looked at him for a moment as he sat down behind a desk and she took the chair in front of him. "How did you hear of me anyway?"

"Bob Bodefeld's mother lives in Louisiana. *Seven Brides for Seven Brothers* is one of her favorite plays, so she went, and when she realized how good you were, she taped a bit of the show . . . which she wasn't supposed to do, but she knew Bob would enjoy watching you act." He shook his head. "Bob knew about this project and thought you might be what we were looking for, so he sent the video to me. After I watched it, I showed my partners. We all wanted to offer it to you then and there, but we had you audition. You beat Sierra out in the last round of auditions, and we were all ready to offer you the part, but she threw a fit and asked her agent to talk to me. Her agent is an old friend, so I agreed to this but told him she couldn't throw any fits. I won't agree to audition her again."

Gabby's eyes widened. "Even if she's right for the part?"

"Even if she's right for the part. The drama that comes along with having her as a member of the cast isn't worth it for me." Steven pushed a contract toward her. "Now, let's talk numbers." He offered her an amount per show that made her gasp. She knew it wasn't what the big stars made, but she really didn't care. It was more than she expected to make as a CPA. "You'll live in a housing unit here on the ranch while we're filming. You can choose to stay here full time or not, but you'll pay for your own lodging when we're not filming. We want you to sign a five-year contract, meaning that if the show does happen to be renewed for a full five years, you'll play the part the entire time. If you happen to become pregnant during that time, we'll either write a baby into the show, or we'll find a way to film around it. Any questions?"

She shook her head. "Those all seem like reasonable expectations to me."

"If you'd like to have your lawyer look over your contract, you're welcome to do so, but we'd like you to be signed on by Wednesday evening at the latest."

"When does filming begin?"

"We're hoping to have all of our ducks in a row within the next ten weeks. You'll need to be on set for at least three weeks prior to that to be fitted for costumes, learn your lines, and get used to the terrain. It's a much higher altitude than you're used to, and we don't want you getting sick from it."

Gabby nodded. "Sounds good. I would like time to look over the contract on my own and make sure I read all the fine print. I may take it to a lawyer in the area if I'm not sure about something."

Steven nodded. "Very wise of you. I'm excited to work with you, Gabby."

"Not half as excited as I am!" Gabby fairly floated out of the office and up to her room. She threw open the curtains and looked out over the ranch, wondering what she'd been so afraid of earlier.

There was a knock at her door, and she hurried over to answer, not sure who to expect. It would be hours before Noah was there for supper . . . well, that might not be true. The man could eat twenty-four hours a day, apparently.

When she opened the door, she stood looking at Sierra, and she forced a smile onto her face. "What can I do for you, Sierra?"

"Who are you sleeping with to get the part? Everyone knows I'm a bigger draw than you are."

"Maybe that's the case, but I fit the part better. They didn't want someone as glamorous or beautiful as you," Gabby said, trying to butter the other woman up. She didn't want a scene. "So they chose me because I will look right at home with dirt smudged on my face."

Sierra wrinkled her nose. "I won't forget this."

Gabby shrugged. "I wouldn't expect you to. I'm sure you'll go right back to Hollywood and get a big part in some movie franchise that will make you millions."

Sierra sniffed. "Of course I will. Who'd want to work at a place like this anyway?" With those words, the actress turned on her heel and walked toward the elevator.

Gabby didn't wait to watch her get on. She had more sense than that. Instead she closed her door and leaned against it.

Walking to her bed, she sat down and read through the contract. It was long and tedious and filled with legalese, but she understood it. When she finished, she laid it on the nightstand. There was nothing unexpected at all. Steven had done a good job explaining it all.

She picked up her phone and dialed a number. "Daddy? I just got offered a contract for the part I want to play. I read over it, and it all looks good to me, but would you mind taking a look? I'd feel better if you did."

"Can you fax it to me? You've got my fax number, right?"

"Of course." She carried one of his cards in her wallet. "I'll see if the front desk will let me fax it. They want a signed contract by Wednesday, but I'd like to get it back to them faster than that."

"Sounds good. You'll have my answer this evening."

"Just text me. I'm going to be out."

"Out?" he asked. "Out with whom?"

Gabby felt herself blushing, and she was glad she hadn't done a Facetime call. Having her father see her blush was not on the agenda for her day. "I'm going to dinner with a friend I've met since I got to the ranch. His name is Noah." She tried to keep her voice calm, but she knew her feelings for the rock climber had to show. He'd already become very special to her.

"All right. Have you told your mother about this Noah?"

"No, Dad. And I don't plan to yet. Right now we're just friends. If there's a reason to talk to her about him, you can bet I will." She took a deep breath. "I'll have this faxed to you within a few minutes. Thanks for your legal expertise." She ended the call, blowing out an exasperated breath. She'd always been overprotected and terribly shy. Now it was catching up with her.

She hurried down to the front desk and talked to the girl who was there. "Is there a fax machine I can use?"

"Yes, of course. How many pages?" The girl's nametag read Jennifer Olson.

Gabby shrugged, holding out the contract. "I'd rather you didn't read it and just sent it if that's possible."

"Of course it is. We guarantee privacy here at River's End Ranch. Do you have a number you want this faxed to?"

"I knew I was forgetting something," Gabby said, grinning. She pulled her father's card from her wallet and handed it to the girl. "The fax number on there. I'll wait to get my papers back."

"Certainly." The girl immediately turned and fed the papers into the machine after pressing a few buttons. The contract was back in her possession five minutes later.

"Thank you so much!"

"My pleasure. I hope you're enjoying your stay."

"I'm convinced this area is what God meant when He talked about paradise. It's absolutely beautiful here!" Gabby glanced out the window behind the front desk. "The mountains and the lake are beautiful separately, but put them together, and I'm sure I'm in heaven!"

"I felt the same way when I first came to the ranch a few months ago," Jennifer said. "I've spent my whole life in a beautiful area of Colorado, but I took it for granted. I wasn't kind, and people there hated me. I came here, and it looks a lot like the area I left, but I feel like I'm getting a second chance, if you know what I mean."

"I do." Gabby smiled at her. "I'm going to be working here for a while. I just got offered the part of Frankie on *Legacy*. I hope we can be friends."

Jennifer's face lit up. "I'd love that. I'm afraid to even reach out to people because I'm afraid my old ugly ways will show. I'm trying hard to change, but it's just not easy."

Gabby covered Jennifer's hand. "Well, we should do lunch sometime soon. Maybe Monday? I'd love to have lunch with you at the café."

"I'd really like that. I'm off Monday, so the timing is good. I'm the new man on the totem pole, so I get weekends, but that's okay."

"I'll see you for lunch Monday then!"

"Let's meet at the café at noon?"

"Perfect!" Gabby hurried to the elevator. She had to look her best for her date with Noah. She only had one dress outfit, and she was already wearing it, but she could do something with her wind-tousled hair and her makeup. Crying about getting your dream role in a television series was not good for your makeup—waterproof mascara or no!

It was less than an hour later when he knocked on her door, and she stood looking at him, a smile on her face. "What is it about you that makes my whole body feel so alive?"

Noah grinned at her. "I like the sound of that!"

She laughed. "Don't get all full of yourself now, Noah. I like you as you are."

"Good. I made reservations at the Italian place. Are you hungry? I'm starving."

"I could eat. I didn't really seem to finish my lunch . . ."

While he drove, she told him about sending the contract to her father to read over. "He'll make sure there are no hidden loopholes or anything else I should know about before I sign it."

"I think that's really smart. You could have taken it to a lawyer near here, but there's no one you'll trust like your father." He pulled into the restaurant parking lot. "I've been excited all day knowing you'll be staying!"

She grinned. "Me too!" Then she remembered Sierra's visit. "Well, maybe not all day." She quickly related everything that Sierra had said to her that day, remembering that he hadn't been around when she'd seen him with Steven either. "And I found out how Steven got the video of my performance in *Seven Brides!*"

"How?"

"Bob Bodefeld's mother sent it to him, and he showed it to Steven, thinking I'd be right for *Legacy.* I'm so glad that worked out! Can you imagine Sierra playing Frankie?" She shuddered at the thought. The girl would not have been able to do the character justice.

"No, I really can't. And I'm not sure how long the ranch would have been able to keep her around without an uprising among the employees. There were already complaints being tossed around about her." Noah leaned over and pressed a kiss to her cheek. "Congratulations."

"Thank you." She looked at him by the lights of the dashboard of the car. "Just so you know, it didn't matter a great deal that I got the part until I met you. After that, I couldn't imagine going home."

He cupped her face, leaning down to kiss her softly. "I didn't much care about the show . . . there's been a lot of excitement about it on the ranch, but until you arrived to be part of it, it didn't matter to me at all. Now, I sure am glad you're staying, Gabby."

"Me too." She snuggled closer to him in the front seat of his truck.

He groaned after a moment. "If we sit here for another minute, we're going to miss our reservation. What are you doing to me, Gabby? I almost forgot food for a minute there!"

Gabby couldn't help but laugh. "Someone or something needs to make you forget about food every once in a while."

He shook his head. "I'll starve to death!"

"I watched you eat six sandwiches for lunch, and then you ate the last two-thirds of mine. I think you're going to make it."

"I'm a growing boy!"

She laughed as he took her hand and pulled her toward the entrance. "We have reservations for two. Noah Andrews," he said.

The hostess checked her list and nodded. "Right this way." They followed her through the restaurant to a quiet corner in the back. "Are you celebrating anything this evening?"

"Yes, we are," Noah said.

"We're celebrating life," Gabby added. She wasn't sure why she wasn't ready to tell the whole world about her new part, but she wanted to keep it close to the chest for a little while yet.

Once they were seated, the hostess asked if they wanted wine, but when they refused, she took the wine glasses away. "You don't drink?" Gabby asked.

He shook his head. "Nope. Never developed a taste for it. You?"

"Not a fan of how it makes me feel." She looked down at the menu, reading over the selections. "Do you want to just order for me? You'll eat most of my meal anyway."

"Aren't you hungry?" he asked, frowning.

"I'm starving. You'll still eat most of my meal!"

He seemed to consider for a moment before nodding. "You're probably right! I do tend to eat more than my share!"

"I hadn't noticed," she said softly, then burst out laughing. "I'm not a good enough actress to pull that off!"

He shook his head at her. "Just think, in a few months when I take you out to eat, you'll be mobbed with people begging for your autograph. You're about to be popular."

It was all Gabby could do not to start singing the words to the song, "Popular" from Wicked. She had been in more than her share of musicals, and she knew the words to a lot of songs from them. "I'm not sure I'm ready for all that."

"I'm not sure it matters if you're ready. If you sign that contract, it's happening. You'll be like a little pebble that starts rolling down a hill.

You won't be able to stop until you reach the bottom—or in this case, the top."

The server came by then and introduced himself as Greg. "Do you want any appetizers this evening?"

Gabby didn't bother to answer. She knew Noah's opinions would be much stronger on this subject than hers.

After they had ordered, he took her hand in his. "I know you're nervous about the whole thing, but I also know you're going to do great. I've heard from a lot of people just how great you did in your audition this morning. They said you and Maynard Butts really had great chemistry." He took a sip of his water. "I'm not sure how I feel about that."

She laughed. "We had great chemistry as siblings. Trust me, there's nothing more to it."

"That's a relief. I worried that you'd have to kiss him for the show!"

"Not at all. They'll eventually bring in someone to play Wally, if the show goes that long, and I'll have to kiss him. It's going to be a family show, so there won't be any 'almost bedroom' scenes, but there will be some kissing going on."

Noah sighed. "I guess I'll have to get used to that idea, won't I?"

"Is there a reason for it to bother you?"

He shrugged. "I'm not sure yet. I'll let you know . . ."

She laughed. "Now you're just toying with my emotions. Very cruel."

"No, I'm guarding my own heart until I'm ready to say how I feel. Very wise of me." He brought her hand to his lips. "I'm just glad that at least for now, you're staying."

Chapter Eight

When Noah dropped her off that evening, Gabby hated the idea of leaving him. She had no idea where they were going. Was he just a vacation fling? Or did he want more the way she did? She couldn't ask. All of her friends had told her that the "Where is this relationship going?" conversation ended relationships faster than anything else could.

He walked her into the main house and escorted her to her room that evening, holding her hand. When they got to her room, he took her keycard and unlocked her door for her. "Thank you for letting me celebrate with you," he said softly, brushing his lips across hers.

"There's no one I would have preferred to celebrate with. I fly home on Wednesday afternoon," she told him, wondering how he'd feel about that.

"But you'll only be gone for a day or two, right? To get your things?"

She shrugged. "I'm really not needed here until three weeks before we start shooting, and that's seven weeks from now. I'm not sure what I'd do here in the meantime." Now that she knew she'd be making a healthy amount of money starting in a few weeks, she could borrow money from her parents to come and stay before then. She hated the idea, but the idea of being without Noah was even worse.

"That long?" Noah frowned. "Whose food am I going to finish when I'm still hungry?" That's not really what bothered him, but he wanted to keep things lighthearted. He didn't want her to realize that she was as important to him as she was.

Gabby frowned. "Maybe there'll be another girl here for a few days who eats like a bird."

He shook his head. "No, I'm going to eat off your plate, or not at all. . . . Wait . . . we both know that's not true! I'm going to eat off your plate or my own. No one else's!"

She laughed. "That makes more sense."

"Do you want to watch a movie tonight? The library here has lots we can borrow."

She was tired, but she wanted every moment with him humanly possible. "I'd really love that."

"Do you want to change into something more comfortable? We have to watch the movies in the library or go through the hassle of checking them out." The truth was he knew that his feelings for her were too strong for them to be alone for long. In the library there was always the risk of someone coming in. He didn't want to accidentally do anything that would make her uncomfortable. She was too precious to him for that.

"Yeah. I have some shorts and a T-shirt that would be perfect for movie watching—unless we have to leave here. Because I might freeze to death if we have to leave here dressed that way."

"Oh, I'd keep you warm," he said, his lips a hair's breath from hers. "Go change. Yes, it's here in the main house." He wanted to kick himself from using the cheesy 'keep warm' line, but she'd seemed to really like it.

He leaned against the wall, waiting for her to change. He could have gone into her room with her and let her change in the bathroom . . . but it didn't seem wise. Not at that moment.

Ten minutes later, they were headed to the library hand-in-hand. He opened the door, and her eyes widened. "Do people know this is here?"

He shrugged. "All the employees know about it. I'm not sure if all the guests do. It's a pretty cool secret, isn't it?"

"What do you want to watch?" she asked, her eyes scanning the titles on the shelves. There were so many movies that she hadn't even heard of on those shelves. They could watch non-stop for a month and never watch anything twice.

"I have no idea. You pick something." He'd be watching her anyway. His feelings for her were so strong. He couldn't bear the idea of her leaving in a few days. Why couldn't she just stay?

She grabbed something from the shelf, not really even looking at the title. It had Julia Roberts on the front, and she'd found you couldn't go wrong with Julia Roberts. Putting the DVD into the player, she moved to the couch and sat down, handing him the remote. She learned early in life that if you were watching a movie with a man, he needed to hold the remote control. It was like he was genetically predisposed for it, and if he wasn't allowed to hold it, his male parts might shrivel up and fall off or something.

Noah took the remote as if it was his due before wrapping his arm around her. If he couldn't keep her there forever, he was going to enjoy every minute with her that he could. *"Notting Hill?* I've never seen this."

"I haven't either. But I love Julia Roberts!"

"We'll see what we think."

She rested her head on his shoulder and was amazed at how quickly the movie flew by. It had her caught between laughter and tears a few times. "I picked good!" she told him when the movie was over.

He grinned at her. The movie had been a romantic comedy, and a decent one as romcoms went, but there were things he'd have rather watched. He'd done as expected, though, and watched her and not the movie. "It wasn't bad."

"I thought it was hilarious when his sister followed Anna into the bathroom and wouldn't quit talking to her and had to be asked to leave when she was unbuttoning her jeans. That girl was a mess." Her eyes were excited and dancing as she told him her favorite part. "What did you like best?"

"Hmm . . . probably when he had to wear goggles to the movie because he couldn't find his glasses." Noah hadn't cared about any of it. She'd been at his side, and that's what was important to him.

She grinned. "That was funny. I'm not sure I'm ready for this night to end. I'm leaving soon, and then we won't be able to spend time together."

"But you'll come back! Soon!" He frowned. "I don't want you to go." He wanted to kick himself, but saying it was probably the only way he could get through the next few days without acting like an absolute lunatic.

She took a deep breath. "I don't want to go. I want to spend the rest of my life right here on this couch with you. How long do you think it would take us to watch all these movies?"

"We could test it and find out. Of course, we'd have to have regular food deliveries. I'm hungry!"

"Already?" She shook her head with a grin. "I guess we can go to the restaurant. I could probably eat a bite or two of a dessert."

"I could eat enough for both of us." Noah got to his feet and held his hand down to her, pulling her to hers. "I'm not going to let myself think about you leaving yet. Instead, I'm going to concentrate on the next three full days we can spend together."

"You're not working?"

"Don't you rain on my parade, Gabby! We'll spend every moment we can together, and it will be wonderful."

"I can go for that." She wanted nothing more than for him to ask her to stay. She knew she had to go home and get her things, but more than anything, she wanted to stay where she was forever. In his arms, she was home.

At the restaurant, he ordered them each a burger and fries. "Only one meal for you?" Avery, the server, asked him. "I've never seen you eat so little."

Noah shrugged. "I'm learning self-control where food is concerned."

Gabby shook her head. "He's already had two-and-a-half dinners, and he's going to eat ninety percent of mine. I might eat a fry."

Dina smiled. "Now that's the Noah we all know and love!"

Gabby studied Noah after Dina left. "Everyone knows and loves you?" She'd thought it was just her.

"Well, the men love me because I take them up on the mountain and show them how to climb it. And what can I say about the ladies? It's not my fault they throw themselves at my feet begging for just a crumb of the three meals I'm eating at any given time."

"Do you ever share a crumb?"

"Not with anyone but you." But with her, he wanted to share everything. She could have the first bite of his burger if she wanted. He wouldn't be happy about it, because the hangries would attack him, but he'd let her do it because he cared that much. That's when it struck him. He cared about her more than he cared about food. She was the woman for him.

Gabby noticed that Noah had suddenly gotten a vacant expression on his face, and she couldn't help but wonder what it was about. "Are you all right? You look like you've seen a ghost."

"No." Well, maybe the ghost of Christmas future. Because now he knew he wanted every Christmas to be spent with her. And every spring and every summer. Forever could never be long enough with the girl beside him. "We should get a piece of the huckleberry pie. Have you ever had huckleberry pie?"

She shook her head. "So huckleberries are real? They're not just the name of a boy who floated down the Mississippi?"

"Not at all. Huckleberry pie is the dessert of Idaho. We're going to have to have a piece to share because I don't want you to feel as if Idaho has slighted you."

"I wouldn't . . ." Gabby studied him a little more, worried about the look she'd seen on his face a moment before. It was gone now, and he seemed to have returned to normal, but she worried about what it meant. Was he thinking about an ex-girlfriend and comparing them? She hoped not!

Soon their burgers were there, and she ate one fry while he plowed his way through the rest. "It's a good thing I like to watch people," she told him. "If we're going to eat out a lot, I have a feeling I won't always be eating when you are."

"I don't usually eat out a ton. It's easier to hide how much you eat if you eat at home more." Noah shrugged. It was one of his secrets for being a foodoholic. Eating at home for most of your meals.

"I never even thought about where you live. Not here on the ranch?"

He shook his head. "I lived here when I first came to the ranch, but now I have a cute little apartment in Riston. You should come to supper tomorrow night, and I'll show you. I'd love to cook for you."

She studied him for a moment, her lips pursed. "Can you cook?"

"I haven't starved to death yet, and that is a testament to my cooking. I don't enjoy cooking a whole lot, not like Bob, but I enjoy eating, and I enjoy being able to pay rent, so I typically cook for myself."

She realized then how much he'd spent on her during her time there. "You need to stop buying my meals. I can get my own!"

Noah shook his head. "That's not what I'm saying at all. I can do this for a week or two. I just don't always live this way." He popped another fry into his mouth. "What about it? Dinner at my place tomorrow?"

"Only if you let me help you cook."

"Can you cook?" he asked, one eyebrow raised.

"I'm no gourmet, but I've never poisoned anyone or burned any kitchens down."

"Then you may be my sous chef for the afternoon. I have my last lesson at two tomorrow, so I'll be done and off the mountain by about three-thirty. May I pick you up then?"

She nodded, wondering what his place would be like. She loved the idea of having an evening just the two of them. "Sounds good to me."

It was only then that Noah realized they would be alone all evening. He wanted to kick himself. They'd watched movies in a public room this evening, just to avoid being alone together, and now they were spending the next evening alone in his apartment. Sometimes he wondered if his brain got clogged by all the food.

They tried the huckleberry pie, and she was surprised at how tart and strong the taste of the berries was. "This is good, but I'm not sure I'd want it again."

Noah shrugged. "It's not my favorite, but I had to let you try something that was all about Idaho." After he paid, he walked her to her room, stopping outside her door for the second time that night. "I guess I really do need to leave you this time."

"I guess so," Gabby said. "It's been a wonderful celebratory day. I couldn't have asked for anything better." She stood on tiptoe and kissed him softly. Her phone had vibrated in her pocket six times in the past fifteen minutes. She was sure it was her father, and he would go a little insane if she didn't answer soon. "Thank you, Noah."

Noah stood outside her door for a little while after she'd closed it. He was falling too fast. There was only one thing he could do, and he'd do it before meeting her for their outing the following afternoon.

Gabby pulled her phone from her pocket just as it started ringing again. "Hi, Daddy."

"Why didn't you answer? I was sure you'd been eaten by a polar bear!"

"There are no polar bears in Idaho, Dad."

"By a grizzly then! Or Bigfoot! I've heard Bigfoot lives in those mountains up there!" Her dad's voice sounded more amused than panicked.

"I'm good. I promise. I was just spending the evening with someone special." She sat down on the edge of her bed and pulled off her socks and shoes. "Did you get a chance to read over the contract?"

"There's nothing in it that you didn't already tell me about. Looks like a standard contract for a television show. You need to be careful not to give away plot until you're told it's allowed and that sort of thing. I'd sign it."

Gabby took a deep breath. "Really? You'd sign?"

"Yes, I really would." He sighed. "It sounds like this means that my baby is going to be spending most of her time in Idaho, filming a television show."

"It does, doesn't it? Can I just say that I'm a little overwhelmed but mostly I'm so excited I can't see straight?"

"Are you excited about the show or the man?"

An hour after they'd hung up, while she was lying in bed, she was still running her father's question through her mind. Was it the show or the man? She wanted both a great deal, and now it seemed as if one was tied up with the other. Would she still have wanted to do the show if Noah wasn't involved, though? Her whole life was about to change. She'd be recognized by strangers on the street. Her name would be a household word, and she would likely be the focal point of gossip in supermarket rags.

She wasn't sure she wanted that part of her new life, but she loved the idea of bringing Frankie to life. The character had such a vitality, even just as part of the written word. Turning her into a living, breathing human who people would admire . . . well, that sounded like something she wanted to spend the rest of her life doing. Yes, it was a little odd to think of herself as famous, but did that matter?

At least she knew that if Noah was falling for her, it wasn't for the money she'd someday make. No, he'd felt emotions for her just as she'd felt them for him. It had all started during their walk through the Old West Town. A place that was part of his life and had been for years. A place that would be part of her future.

Her last thoughts as she fell asleep that night were that she and Noah would get used to her new popularity together as a couple. They would have to make the most of the short time they had left before the show aired. She didn't want to be stopped every time she left the house by paparazzi.

Chapter Nine

Noah went to church at the little chapel on the ranch, surprised to see Gabby there. They'd never really talked about God and religion, but he should have realized she was a believer, just by the way she talked and acted.

After the service, she walked over to him and smiled. "I guess we can just start our afternoon now."

Noah shook his head slowly. "Actually, I need a little bit of time. Can I pick you up at one as we planned?" He didn't want to admit it, but he needed to walk over to Jaclyn's house and talk to her. He prayed the fairies were communicating with her again because he needed their wisdom to know what to do.

"Oh?" Gabby looked hurt at his answer, but he couldn't explain. Not yet. "You don't have to spend the day with me if you don't want to."

"You know I want to spend every day with you forever. I'm not trying to push you off, there's just a little errand I need to run . . . alone."

"Ranch business?" she asked, wondering what it could possibly be. He'd not tried to push her away before, and it felt awful.

"No, it's personal. I promise, it's not bad. I'll see you at one. Is that all right?" he asked.

"Oh, sure. That's fine. We're going to lunch?" she asked.

"I thought we'd go to lunch, and then we'll spend some more time on snowmobiles. I got you your own this time."

Gabby shook her head. "I'm not ready for my own." She was, but she was more ready to sit on the back of his with her arms wrapped around him. He made her feel so safe.

"That's fine then. I'll return yours. I'll come to your room to get you at one." He glanced at his phone and saw that it was eleven. That gave him two hours to get to Jaclyn's and wade through whatever she told him about his future with Gabby. He badly needed advice because he was ready to buy a ring and drop to one knee, just to get her to not stay long when she went back to Louisiana. He wasn't sure that was exactly the right reason to propose to a woman. He leaned down and kissed her cheek. "I'll see you in a couple of hours."

She frowned after him as he left, wondering what was going on with him. "Something wrong?" a voice asked from behind her.

Gabby turned to see Jennifer standing there. "Oh, hi! I'm just trying to figure out what's going on in Noah's brain, but he's a man, so I'm sure it's not figure outable."

"Of course it's not. Where are you headed now?" Jennifer asked.

Gabby had a hard time believing people in Jennifer's old home hadn't liked her. "I have no idea. Noah is picking me up at one for lunch, but that gives me two hours to spin my wheels."

Jennifer smiled at that. "Did you get a response to your fax yesterday?"

"Yes! It was the contract for the lead in *Legacy,* and I was sending it to my father, who's a lawyer. He told me to sign. He thinks it's all in my favor."

"Oh, that's great." Jennifer started walking toward the main house, and Gabby fell into step beside her. "There's something awfully special about this place."

"You said you'd grown up somewhere similar?"

Jennifer nodded. "I did, but it didn't have the big family atmosphere, at least not for me. I grew up in Silver Springs, Colorado, and while it was a beautiful place, I never really fit in like I should have."

"Any idea why? Was it too cliquey?"

"Not at all." Jennifer sighed. "You want to know the dirty truth about me?"

Gabby frowned. "Only if you want to tell me."

"Well, the town I grew up in was formed by a family that lived there. The people from that family were like town royalty, and I was always eaten up with jealousy. I did really mean things to the girls in the family—they were actually all cousins—because I was interested in one of them boys in the family. Crazy huh?"

"Really?" Gabby asked. She couldn't imagine the pretty girl beside her being cruel to people.

"Oh, really. I went after every man who dated one of the girls. I went after every one of the men in the family. I said some cruel things. I hired one of the girls to do an anniversary party for my parents, and I was just rude and ugly." Jennifer sighed. "Their family and mine were the richest people in town, and I was sure we should marry to combine dynasties or some such nonsense."

"I think it's good you left."

"It really is. They're all married now. All ten of the cousins, and they're all happy. I was watching them all and getting more and more jealous of their happiness. My parents owned an inn, and they made me train under two of the cousins, and I hated them for it. The cousins, not my parents. Now I'm really good at what I do, and I'm glad I'm here, working and doing the things I'm good at. I just don't have to prove anything because they're not around."

"Well, you sure don't have to prove anything to me!" Gabby said with a grin. "I'm just a Southern girl trying to figure out how I'm going to live in Northern Idaho for the next year or so as we work on this show."

"Only a year or so?"

Gabby grinned. "Okay, so the contract is for five years. They have the right to ask me not to do any other movies or shows if they interfere with my filming schedule. I'm so excited."

"I'm glad! Have you signed the contract yet?"

"No, I haven't. Do you know when Steven Pickman checks out?"

"He checks out on Wednesday," said a voice behind her.

Gabby jumped, turning to see Steven standing there. "I'm going to sign the contract. My father looked over it, and he said I should sign if it's what I want to do. And it is. I want to be Frankie!"

Steven smiled. "I'm glad to hear it. Do you want to give it to me now, so we won't have to worry about it later?"

Gabby nodded. "Let me run to my room and get it. I'll be back in a minute."

Jennifer went to the elevator with her. "I've never watched anyone sign a contract for a major part in a television show. Do you mind?"

Gabby laughed. "I don't mind, but I don't feel like I'm important enough for you to want to watch me sign a contract."

"You will be!" Jennifer told her with a grin. "I have a feeling this show is going to steal the hearts of the country. So many people have been here and feel like they belong here. They'll all watch it, and they'll tell their friends, who will tell their friends. . . . You'll be bigger than Valerie Savoy by this time next week!"

"I have a feeling you're wrong about that. I love Valerie Savoy, and I don't want to be bigger than her. I think I'll be just fine floating along doing my own thing as the star of the show." Gabby opened her door and found the contract in the corner. She quickly signed her name to the bottom of it and dated it. "Let's take this down to Steven. Then he only has to worry about getting his hero to sign on."

"Do you know who they chose for that?" Jennifer asked.

"Yeah, Maynard Butts. Do you know him?"

"No idea who he is!"

"Well, I liked him a lot when we ran through lines together. He's going to play my brother, so there will be no awkward kissing scenes for at least a year or two."

"Are you in love with Noah?" Jennifer asked.

Gabby blushed. "You know what? I think I might be. I've only known him for a few days, though. Is it possible to fall in love with someone you've known for such a short period of time?"

"I think so," Jennifer said. "I think you two look really good together. He's a nice guy, and you're a nice person, too. Together, you'll make nice kids and be happy."

Gabby frowned. "You didn't have feelings for Noah, did you?"

Jennifer shook her head. "Not for Noah, but I so badly want to settle down. Deep inside me I have this feeling that I'm absolutely unlovable. I need to be loved."

Gabby hugged Jennifer. "As your new friend, I declare you very lovable. You know . . . there's a woman on the ranch right now. I met her Thursday evening at trivia. Her name is Dr. Lachele, and she introduces people at the altar. I wonder if you could talk to her and get her to find someone for you."

"Are you saying that the only way I could get a man to marry me is if he didn't see me before I walked down the aisle toward him?"

Gabby's eyes widened, and she felt terrible. "No, of course not! I was just trying to mention an alternative. . . ."

Jennifer laughed. "I knew you were. I was just teasing you. I think I'd like to meet her. Are we still doing lunch tomorrow?"

"Yes! Do you want me to see if she'll meet us there?"

"That would be wonderful. I can't believe how much I like the idea of meeting a man after I have said 'I do.' It really sounds like the perfect solution for me."

"When I first met her, I wondered if anyone took her up on it. I can see they do!"

Jennifer shrugged. "I don't know if it makes me desperate, but I do know I make a bad first impression with men. I'm going to give it a try. Why not?"

"Doesn't bother me. I'm here to support you!"

"You'll have to be my maid of honor."

It was with those words that Gabby really understood the extent of this girl's inability to make friends. She wanted to hug her and tell her they'd be friends forever. "I would love to!" Though she really hoped it would be matron by then. Of course, she had no idea how quickly Dr. Lachele worked.

NOAH SUCKED IN A DEEP breath before approaching Jaclyn's house. He didn't want to have to talk to her, but he knew it was time. No one on the ranch married without first going through Jaclyn. He knocked on her door and held his breath, hoping she wouldn't be home.

When the door opened, he jumped back. "Dr. Lachele?"

"Get in here, boy. We know you want to talk about pretty little Gabby. You ready to propose yet?" Dr. Lachele asked him.

He went inside, looking around for Jaclyn. When he didn't see her, he stood there for a moment, wondering what to do. "Is Jaclyn not home?"

"Yeah, she's outside making up little bowls of honey for the fairies, trying to get back into their good graces. She's no good at matchmaking without their help, apparently. I keep telling her to just follow her gut, but she ignores me." Dr. Lachele waved toward the couch. "Move a rabbit so you can sit. Have you ever seen this many bunnies in your life?"

The door opened, and Jaclyn stepped in. "Are you still complaining about the bunnies, Lachele? I don't know what your problem is. Everyone in the world loves bunnies but you."

"I love bunnies . . . I just don't know that I love being buried alive in them!" Dr. Lachele nodded toward Noah. "He's here to talk about Gabby."

"Well, of course he is. I told you it was Gabby for him."

"I believe *I* told *you* it was Gabby for him."

Jaclyn sighed. "What does it matter as long as we both agree that it's Gabby for him?"

"No idea." Dr. Lachele sat down in a chair after moving a bunny. "Tell us what's on your mind, Noah."

Noah looked back and forth between the two women. It was hard enough to tell one person how he felt, but two? It helped him that they were both a bit crazy, so maybe people wouldn't believe them if they talked about this. "Is this conversation confidential?" he finally asked.

"Does it need to be?" Jaclyn asked, taking her seat. "I didn't make cookies and tea for you. If you need some, let me know, otherwise get on with it."

Noah frowned. Everyone talked about how she always had snickerdoodles and tea ready, and he felt left out. "I do probably need some snickerdoodles and tea."

Jaclyn nodded at Dr. Lachele. "You get the tea. You know where I keep the snickerdoodles."

"How long have you two been friends?" Noah asked. It felt like they had known one another forever when he watched them.

Jaclyn frowned. "I don't know. A day or two? How long have you been here, Lachele?"

"I got here Thursday, but I met you Friday!"

"We've known each other since Friday. Now, why are you really here?" Jaclyn was watching him carefully, her eyes wide. "You know you can tell me."

"Well, you were right. It's about Gabby."

Dr. Lachele let out a whoop in the kitchen. "Told you it was her!"

"I told you!" Jaclyn yelled back. When she saw the look on Noah's face, she smiled. "Now, what about Gabby?"

Noah wondered how many times he'd be interrupted, but he decided he didn't care. He was going to say what he needed to say. When the cookies appeared on a plate in front of him, he grabbed one and instantly felt better. He didn't even need to eat it as long as he was touching it. "Well, Gabby got the part she wanted on *Legacy,* and I'm thrilled for her. I want her to stay on the ranch, and this way she can."

"That sounds like it's good news," Jaclyn said.

"Oh, it really is. The only problem is that I don't want her to even go home to pack her things. She doesn't need to be here on the ranch for filming for another seven weeks. How am I supposed to wait seven weeks?"

Jaclyn grinned. "Well, the way I see it is you have two options. You can wait that seven weeks, pining away for her, wondering if she's found another man while she's gone. Or you can ask her to marry you now and marry her before she leaves. Then she'll come back faster."

"I can't ask a woman I just met on Thursday to marry me!"

"My dear boy, how long have you worked at River's End Ranch?" Jaclyn asked.

"About ten years, I think." Noah shook his head. "What does that have to do with anything?"

"Haven't you watched how fast people get married on this ranch? It's almost like there's something in the water. Of course, a lot of it has to do with the help the fairies provide me to help others." Jaclyn smiled not-so-modestly.

"I'm sure that's a lot of it," Noah said obediently. "So you don't think it would be a problem to just go and propose to her?"

"Not if you have a ring. Do you have a ring?" Jaclyn eyed him suspiciously.

"Well, not yet. I only met her Thursday. How many times do I have to tell you that?" Noah was sure he was dealing with crazy people, but now that he'd started, he was afraid to stop.

"So go get one during your lunch hour tomorrow. The fairies say she's having lunch with someone else."

"So the fairies are talking to you again?" Dr. Lachele asked excitedly.

"Well, they just did, but don't hold your breath. They're pretty finicky creatures. I never know if they're going to talk to me from one minute to the next." Jaclyn sighed. "Why can't the leprechauns be the ones helping me? They like to play practical jokes, but at least they don't get their feelings hurt at the drop of a hat."

"So you're telling me that if I go buy her a ring during my lunch tomorrow, and I ask her to marry me, that's my best answer?" Noah asked.

Jaclyn shook her head. "I told you that you have two choices. Which choice you make is completely up to you. The fairies and I don't tell people what to do. We give them choices."

Noah was sure he'd heard about her flat out telling people what to do, but he was afraid to argue with her. He took a deep breath. "So now I'm supposed to contemplate which is the right answer?"

"Sounds like the logical conclusion, doesn't it?" Jaclyn asked.

Noah looked over at Dr. Lachele, who was sitting quietly, having only eaten one of the snickerdoodles because Noah had polished off the rest. "Do you agree?"

"That you need to make your own decisions? Of course, I do. I don't tell people what to do any more than the fairy lady here does. I will tell you that I think you're stupid if she doesn't have a ring on her finger before she gets on that plane to go back to Louisiana, but I won't tell you what to do."

Jaclyn nodded. "Very stupid. Imbecilic really."

Noah sighed. "All right. I guess I'm spending my lunch hour tomorrow buying a ring."

"Why do you sound upset about it?" Dr. Lachele asked. "I thought you came here to talk about how much you loved her and couldn't let her go."

"I did. And I do love her, and I can't imagine spending the rest of my life without her."

"So what's the problem?" Jaclyn asked.

"I've never eaten her cooking! What if I starve? Can I come here and get cookies if she can't cook?" Noah asked.

"I'll send you care packages if necessary. Just go marry the woman!" Dr. Lachele waved him toward the door, and he stood up, carefully avoiding two gray bunnies who seemed to be kissing each other. Did bunnies kiss? He had no idea, but those two seemed to be.

"How many bunnies do you have, Jaclyn?" Noah asked as he walked toward the door.

"I'm a matchmaker, a fairy whisperer, and a bunny keeper. I'm *not* a mathematician!" Jaclyn closed the door firmly behind him, and he heard her laughing as he walked away. She was odd, but everyone trusted her to do the right thing where matchmaking was concerned.

He rubbed the back of his neck as he checked the time. "I'll have to do it during lunch. I need to be at her room in ten minutes." He broke into a run, not certain how Gabby felt about men being late for dates.

Chapter Ten

Noah picked Gabby up for lunch at one as he'd promised. They drove the short distance into Riston in silence. Finally, when they were almost there, she asked, "How was your meeting?"

"What meeting?" Noah asked, thoroughly confused.

"I got the impression you were meeting someone after church." She watched him carefully for a reaction.

"Oh, that. It was enlightening, confusing, and very frustrating, but I made it through." He stopped the truck in front of the Chinese place in town. "I hope you like Chinese. I'm about to order eight meals."

"Eight?"

"Yeah, I've been nervous. Being nervous consumes a lot of energy!"

Gabby laughed. If there was one thing she could always count on, it was the fact that he would always be hungry. "If you had just been eating at an all-you-can-eat buffet, and someone came to your house with a pizza to share, would you share it?"

"That depends."

"On what?" she asked.

"On whether the pizza had anchovies. I can't abide anchovies." He took her hand and walked into the place with her. After ordering more than any one person could possibly eat, he looked at her. "What do you want?"

"Couldn't I just have a little bit of each of your meals?" she asked. He really had ordered eight full meals for himself. She found Chinese food to be overly filling to begin with.

He frowned. "Why don't I order one more meal, and then you can share?"

Gabby sighed. "All right. I won't eat a whole meal anyway."

"I know you won't. I think it's what I love most about you." As soon as the words were out of his mouth, Noah bit his tongue. He hadn't meant to declare his love for her in the middle of a Chinese restaurant in Riston. He'd planned to take her up onto the mountain and sweetly tell her how he felt.

"Oh?" she asked. She didn't know what else to say. Was she supposed to tell him she loved him, too? What kind of a declaration of love was that anyway! It was almost insulting. Of course, he was a man who loved food, so it wasn't completely surprising.

He shrugged. "Well, you don't eat my food. Of course that makes me happy."

After lunch, they went back to the ranch, and he took her up onto the mountain again. He stopped at the place where they'd picnicked because it was time for a snack. As he ate a bag of nuts, he asked, "Are you up for going a little higher?"

Gabby thought about it and realized she really wasn't at all nervous. "Yeah, I think we can go higher. As long as I get to keep holding onto you."

He walked to her, tilting her chin up for a kiss. "As far as I'm concerned, you never have to let go."

On the machine, he started up the mountain again, carefully staying on the mountain side of the path, so she wouldn't be nervous about falling. When they got to the place he'd wanted to take her to, he carefully stopped and got off, holding his hand out to her. "From here, you can see the whole empire. I love to look out over the whole ranch and know I have access to all those places. I'm part of this dynasty."

She put her hand in his, taking deep breaths to quell her fears. "What if I'm too afraid to look out?"

"You won't be. You're here on the ranch to face your fears. I promise you, I'll be with you every single step of the way." He led her to about five feet from the edge. There was no danger there. "Look."

Gabby gazed out over the ranch, her heart stopping in her chest for a moment. "It's so beautiful! Is the whole lake on ranch property?"

"It is. I have a feeling you'll be washing clothes in that lake at times."

She grinned. "Banging them on a rock to get them clean."

"I wanna see that." He wrapped his arms around her from behind. "I don't want you to be afraid, but you needed to see this place. You need to know that you can be up here and not have a panic attack."

She took in the view for another moment before turning in his arms, wrapping her arms around his neck. "You know something, Noah?"

"What?"

"I think you're pretty incredible. Thank you for helping me to face my fears."

"Haven't you figured out yet that I'd do anything for you?"

DURING HIS LUNCH THE following day, Noah drove into Riston to the jewelry store there. Despite how he'd made things sound to her, he was no pauper. He wasn't rich, but he had a nice healthy savings account, and he couldn't wait to put the perfect ring on her finger.

He looked into the cases, knowing he didn't look like he had any right to even be shopping in a store like this. He was covered in mud and snow from his morning on the mountain, but there was no time to change before his jewelry shopping.

"Can I see that one?" he asked the man behind the counter, who immediately nodded and took out the ring he wanted to see.

"Is this for an engagement?" the man asked.

"It is. She's the most beautiful girl in the world, and she has the biggest greenest eyes I've ever seen."

"May I make a suggestion then?"

"Please! I've never even imagined being in a jewelry store shopping for an engagement ring!"

"Most men haven't." The man slid another ring out from the case, holding it out to him. "If her eyes are green, there's a good chance she enjoys wearing that color to bring out her eyes. So I would get this one. There's still a large diamond solitaire, but this one is surrounded by tiny emeralds instead of diamonds. She'll know you were thinking about her tastes when you chose it. And it's five hundred less than the other ring you first chose."

"Does that mean it's not as good?" Noah asked. "She deserves the best!"

"Oh, no, of course not. It just means that most people think they need just diamonds in an engagement ring. Dare to be different and get her something that suits her." The man looked at Noah for a moment. "Do you have a picture of her?"

Noah fished his phone out of his pocket. "I took a selfie with her on the mountain last night." He showed the man the photo.

"She is very beautiful. Definitely the emeralds."

"All right." Noah pulled his debit card from his wallet. "Let's do this thing?"

"Will you be needing financing?" the man asked.

"Nope. I've got a debit card, and I know how to use it."

GABBY'S LUNCH WITH Jennifer and Dr. Lachele was interesting, but she was happy to have a couple of hours alone before it was time for Noah to pick her up for the evening. She only had one more day to spend with him before she needed to go back to Louisiana. Then seven weeks without seeing him at all. She wasn't sure how that would work for her. She'd never been in love. She'd never even had crushes like all her friends in school. She'd always been the most level-headed girl she knew about men. And now here she was, eating her heart out for a man who climbed rocks for a living.

She dressed carefully, but she had little to wear with her that he hadn't seen. In the end, she put on a pair of jeans and a casual T-shirt. When she heard the knock, she grabbed her sweater and jacket and pulled both on. Opening the door, she saw Noah leaning in the doorway. "Hi, you."

"Hi." He caught her hips and pulled her to him, kissing her. "Can you handle one quick ride up the mountain before we go to my place for supper?"

"Sure. But you won't starve to death?"

"I have emergency rations. Three bags of beef jerky, a big bag of Cheetos, and six bottles of water. I think we're going to be fine."

She grinned at him, shaking her head. "We don't have long before it's dark. Is it safe?"

"We'll hurry." He knew he couldn't take her to the spot where he'd let her look out over the ranch the night before, but he could take her to their picnic spot. Surely that would be almost as good.

They got to the front, and he climbed onto one of the machines sitting there, and she got on after him, snuggling close. She loved the snowmobile because it meant she had the right to wrap her arms around him, and no one thought a thing of it.

As they rode up the trail, she rested her cheek on his shoulder, glorying in being close to him. She loved him more than she'd ever dreamed she could love a man, and she would leave for seven weeks in two days. There was no way she wasn't going to make the most of the time she had left with him.

When they reached the picnic area, he led her to the overlook, and they both looked down on the ranch. The view wasn't as spectacular as it was from the spot he'd taken her to do the day before, but it was still nothing short of breathtaking. "I've lived here for ten years, and I love this ranch. It's in my blood as much as it is in the Westons.'"

"I can see that." Why was he telling her this?

"I don't ever plan to leave River's End. I'll retire from this place an old man. If you want to have someone in your life who sits behind a desk, I'm not him." Noah felt the need to warn her that he was never going to change occupations. He loved what he did, and he wasn't going to change that.

"I understand. I'm glad you've found what makes you happy. So many people haven't."

"You don't mind that I climb rocks and teach people to ski for a living?" He watched her face as she answered.

"Why would I mind?"

"So you wouldn't mind being married to a man who has no desire to do anything but physical labor for the rest of his life?"

Her heart started thumping in her chest, going wild. "Noah? Are you trying to ask me something?"

He pulled the ring box out of his pocket and held it out to her. "I listened to the guy in the store when he told me you'd like emeralds surrounding the diamond, but there is a diamond. If you don't like it, I can take it back!"

She opened the box and gasped. "I love emeralds. I wear green all the time!" Her eyes met his. "I can't answer a question that hasn't been asked."

He took a deep breath, pressing her fingers to his lips. "I love you with everything inside me, and I know we've only known each other a few days, but I think we need to get married. I can't bear to let you go. Gabriella Tanner? Would you do me the honor of being my wife?"

Gabby felt a tear drift down her cheek as she nodded. "Yes, I'll marry you! My parents will think I'm crazy, but I don't care. I love you, too, Noah Andrews!"

He wrapped both arms around her and lifted her off her feet, spinning her in a circle. "Now?"

"Now? You mean marry you right this minute?"

"Tomorrow would be good enough. Pastor Kevin is used to crazy fast weddings around here."

Gabby bit her lip. "Saturday. I'll call my parents. Mom will pack my things, and they can be here for the wedding." She knew Jennifer would have to be her maid of honor. After the talk they'd had the previous day, the woman was better in her corner than out of it.

"I guess I can wait until Saturday . . . it does seem like an awfully long time away, though!"

She pressed her lips to his. "We can make it that long. If it's true love, it lasts for *more* than a week."

"A lifetime is all I ask."